SHELTERED

Part 1 Of The Sinking Man Series

Justin S. Leslie

J.S.L

Paperback ISBN: 978-1-7331873-7-4
eBook ISBN: 978-1-7331873-6-7

Contact Information email: Abaddonbooks@hotmail.com

Facebook: @Maxabaddonbooks

Website: www.JustinLeslie.com

"Death is not the greatest loss in life. The greatest loss is what dies inside while still alive."

TUPAC SHAKUR

NOTE FROM THE AUTHOR

If you're reading this, you probably already know about my Max Abaddon books. The following is a zombie short series based in Northeast Florida, as are all my stories.

It's not your typical fare in this space. Yes, the zombies are the problem, not exactly everyone you run into. The series will have several short novellas released throughout the year and is geared toward TV adaptation. Think of each short novella as an episode.

CHAPTER 1

Ben stood looking out over the St. Johns River from his secluded dock. Like most mornings, he held his cup of coffee in one hand and half-cocked attitude on life in the other. The out-of-the-way gated community he lived in, tucked away in a small inlet, secluded him from the apocalypse that was raging around him. At least, raging last time he had checked, which had been never.

Ben's morning walk didn't require him to wear pants — or underwear, for that matter — anymore. He leaned over with the robe he wore lightly pushed out of the way and released a splashing torrent, peeing directly into the water.

The 9mm Glock hanging off a shoulder holster was the one thing he never forgot to wear. Pants yes, gun no.

Reaching down, Ben turned on the one thing he had that connected him to the world outside of his secluded, empty riverfront neighborhood: a satellite phone. He sighed, taking a sip of his coffee before shaking his head.

"Hello," was all he said into the receiver after dialing the last number he had called — the phone number his wife, Sarah, had given him before leaving. He'd learned that keeping the phone on all the time in hopes of receiving a call from her would only run the battery down over time, so with this knowledge, he only turned it on every morning while walking out to the dock, also sending a short text.

Two months ago to the day, he had received a text message saying nothing more than, "The plan...safe." That message had reenergized Ben after almost ten months of complete seclusion.

The plan was simple. Anything ever happened, they made their way home, no matter who was out or where they were. The funny thing about apocalypses was that they had a peculiar sense of irony. Ben had struggled at first to figure out a name for what was happening, so he had hit the easy button and landed on zombies.

When it had first started, the world was calling them crazies. People catching a disease, then losing their shit. That had changed, though, and for the worse. People had started shifting and becoming, well...zombies of a sort.

Sarah, Ben's wife, worked for the CDC and had been called to work the case. Only this time, it hadn't been the regular routine of being gone for just a few weeks; this time, it had been months. She had gone to Denver and would go radio silent for weeks at a time. Meanwhile, the world had started to burn.

First, it had been in the news. So-called experts telling everyone to stay calm, only to have the news report rising numbers of infected at a staggering pace. In an effort to stop the spread, certain groups of people and areas had been slowly isolated, the full quarantine starting only a few weeks later. Only essential personnel had been allowed to function, slowly eroding the world's economies.

Soon, the general population had become restless, leading to riots and, what turned out even worse, people going back to their normal everyday lives out of necessity. The number of cases rose uncontrollably, overwhelming the health care system and collapsing it. This had only taken a few short months.

Before the world stopped, it was reported that a trial vaccine had caused the virus to change and mutate. Infected people — crazies — upon their imminent death, changed to something even worse, something dead. When the vaccine proved unsuccessful, the evacuations began.

As a biomedical doctor, part of Sarah's job was to have a family care plan while she was away. Ben and Sarah had often binge-watched "Elite Preppers," a show for rich people that could afford to truly prep.

That faithful night six months before the shit hit the fan and she had been called away, the two of them had drunk multiple bottles of wine. Ben hated the stuff, but it always put the two in a mood for trouble. During a commercial break, an advertisement selling three years' worth of supplies and survival gear had appeared.

It had also included a full solar kit and backup system for the house. All yours for the ripe old price of thirty thousand dollars. That night, they had bought the kit and mapped out their plans in case something ever did go down.

Ben let out a breath thinking about that night, taking the final sip of his coffee before sprinkling the rest on the ground. He turned, looking at the house as he did every morning. He fondly thought about the two of them calling the next day to cancel the order, only to find it nonrefundable, the effects of wine not in the cancelation policy.

Their house was nice by any standards a doctor would have. At five thousand square feet, it had plenty of room for what they had hoped would be a soon-to-grow family. As they were both in their mid-thirties, the clock had been ticking.

The solar panels gleamed off the back of the house, catching Ben's attention. Since they couldn't get a refund on the drunken purchase, the two had decided to go all the way, adding a water filtration system to the list of upgrades.

The house had been made for this. "How ironic," Ben said to the air.

The neighborhood itself was relatively small, owning five other similarly large houses. It was a gated community and designed to not draw attention to its semi-wealthy owners, which included an ex-athlete, a local attorney, a retired couple whose house I had to visit yet, and a retired admiral.

The turnoff was on a shaded two-lane road on the east side of the St. Johns River, south of the Buckman Bridge and Jacksonville, Florida.

If you didn't know the small neighborhood was there, you would miss the unimproved lane leading down to its entrance.

The gate was ten feet tall, made of plaster block, and it wrapped around to the water's edge.

What made this property even better was that the houses sat back in a small cove, with docks at the back of each house only large enough to park a medium-sized ski boat. The trees, after not being maintained, had started to grow together at the opening of the cove. You could still see the houses, but if you weren't looking and passed by on a boat, you more than likely would miss the collection of nice households altogether.

When the evacuations had started, Ben had elected not to leave per their plan, staying put instead. This had ended up being the best possible scenario, since a couple of weeks later, he'd heard jets overhead and what appeared to be bombs dropping in the area near Naval Air Station Jax, which had been the evacuation hub for the First Coast.

Sarah had always insisted on not leaving home in the case of a mass infection. "Large masses of people are always a bad idea, and I wish people would stop doing it," rang in Ben's head as he walked up the final steps to the house.

In all fairness, it had taken several months for Ben to even feel the effects of the devastation around. Money could make even the end of the world a little more tolerable.

He was in a reflective mood. Maybe it was the fact that he was going to go through another house today. To date, he had only been through two others. The whole thing about, the devil next door had ended up taking on a true meaning after what he had found in one house, but that was for another day.

His neighbors had left on the first day of the evacuations, hoping to get a front-row seat to wherever it was they were going. Ben was betting on them never making it off the base. Television signals had been cut off later that week, leaving the rest up to Ben's imagination; only the noises he heard in the night being carried over the water, which could be from miles away, let him know anything about the outside world.

The watch on Ben's wrist came to life. "Good morning," the chirpy electronic voice of his smartwatch pronounced.

Ben pulled the watch to his mouth. "Morning. Set an alarm for noon. Label it 'house.'" The watch was the latest technology had to offer. It was programmable, and he had even sprung for the upgraded artificial intelligence application.

Luckily for Ben, it didn't need the Internet. All he had to do was plug it into the computer and answer three hundred questions. The watch programmed itself from there. You could even adjust it to respond certain ways to phrases.

Set in his routine, Ben reprogrammed the conversation every month with simple phrases, that while scripted, made time pass.

"How are you?"

"I'm fine."

"Good. What are you doing today?"

"I'm going to the house at the end of the street."

"Stay safe."

It was his own private Wilson. It also had a few other neat functions, like a heart rate monitor that told him when he was too excited, and reminders for when to eat and take a nap. Ben could even control certain functions of the house from the device.

It had become his partner in crime. He had even given it a British woman's accent. He had an odd relationship with it in some sick yet acceptable way. Her name was Eve.

For this little chat, the watch had been programmed to say good morning between set hours when his heart rate elevated to a certain level, which usually meant after coffee.

Walking into the house, Ben set down the mug before heading off for a shower. He often found himself feeling guilty for how nice things were. Warm running water, power, and a lot of booze stashed away.

Ben's mind wandered as it often did toward thoughts of Sarah, filling his mind with memories of her under the sprinkling water of the shower. He wondered where she was, and if she was safe. Would she still love him when she got back? All the bullshit couples thought about when they were apart.

Something was bothering Ben, however. Time was moving forward, and Sarah was not home yet. Over time, Ben had taken a few maps, and with the help of some old college math textbooks he had found in storage, he had figured out how long it would take for her to get back.

It was one of the first things he had done when all communication with the outside world had been cut. The calculations had included stops, incidents, and weather. The time was getting close. He had predicted it would take her roughly a year if she didn't travel by vehicle.

He figured vehicles were probably off the table, as he hadn't heard more than a handful over the year. After watching one too many zombie movies, he wasn't going to poke around to find out.

Ben, again following his daily routine, walked over to his map and calendar and marked off another day. Tomorrow would be in the red zone, as he called it. He projected she would be close soon. Thoughts of leaving out signs crossed his mind, letting Sarah know he was in fact, there. He would figure that piece out soon.

Today marked eleven months and fifteen days since the world as he knew it had ended. She had been gone several months prior to that point, and he had counted every day since the last full call he had received from her shortly after the evacuations had started toward the one-year mark.

The message he had received a few months ago justified everything he was doing.

Showered and shaved, Ben went into the master bedroom, laying out his equipment for the day. It included protective clothing, combat boots, and general items he may need in case of an emergency, including some type of weapon.

Ben looked at himself in the mirror. His face was attractive, strong, and kempt. The exercise and healthy living, for the most part, had treated him well over the past year. The light scar above his right eye stood out on an otherwise   blank canvas.

He lightly combed his hair back, pulling it behind his ears. While he usually kept it trimmed, he had decided to let it grow out last fall. Years of healthy living had covered up the tough years of his oftentimes troubled youth.

The light smell of the approaching fall hung in the air,

accompanied by the scent of a burning vanilla candle. Sarah was one of those candle types. She had candles for every season and occasion, from date night to afternoon cocktails with friends, which always ended up being experienced through smell.

While Ben had power, it wasn't enough to run the house fully. He could run the AC, but to the detriment of other systems, so he ran it sparingly. As was the case most days, he opened the windows, ran the fans, and let Mother Nature do all the work as he prepared to leave.

Even though Ben knew the neighborhood was empty, he was always cautious when leaving the main property. As he did on these occasions, Ben talked through his routine.

"Jeans, yup. Long sleeve undershirt, yup. Boots, ahh...these will do for today," Ben said, pulling out the new tan combat boots — which just happened to be a perfect fit that he had found in the admiral's house next door.

It also happened to be where he had acquired a semiautomatic M4 assault rifle with all the fixings, a lightweight plate carrier to attach things on, and his favorite scavenged item so far: one of those big ass Rambo-looking knives.

The pistol he carried around was actually his, and also a rather nice hunting rifle, but on the tactical side of things, his defense was far inferior to that of his neighbor's.

The only thing better, in his opinion, was the stockpile of steroids he had found in Jake's house, the ex-football player. Ben had decided to spend some time bulking up, and after studying the books he had also found stashed, decided to fill his body with the muscle-building chemicals.

He had always thought those supplements were supposed to make you go all crazy. Nothing could have been further from the truth. When taken properly, and the proper type, he felt rejuvenated.

Altogether, Ben had packed on fifteen pounds of muscle, stopping a few months back as the book recommended. Plus, he was sure their shelf life would soon run out, and didn't want to risk it.

He often dreamed of Sarah blushing when she saw him again.

After a few more minutes of prep, Ben headed downstairs, grabbing the keys to his prior-athlete neighbor's Toyota Tacoma. He had pulled it into his garage as one of a handful of exit routes in case his Tesla couldn't make it.

The Toyota was a hybrid and didn't care if it drank gas or electricity, but the fuel was still usable, and he had a stock of stabilizer he had gathered from the other boat owners. By his measure, including the latest developments in gas, the fuel would last roughly two to three years, maybe a little longer if he could manage it.

Over the past five years, almost half the cars on the road were electric. That, however, created a whole other level of shit-stirring problems.

While fuel would last for years if stored properly, getting a stable current of electricity outside of his domain was going to be an issue.

Either way, it was time for Ben to leave his personal paradise and go through the last house in the neighborhood.

CHAPTER 2

This house was roughly the same size as Ben's; however, it was a more traditional Craftsman style. The loop around the cove was roughly a quarter-mile, which meant there was plenty of space between the properties. The three in the middle were closer, while the homes on the end such as this one, were more separated.

Even though Ben was well stocked with the necessary supplies to last for several years, he wanted to ensure he had everything within his kingdom at his disposal. He figured the more he found close to home, the less chance of him having to ever leave. This was fine with Ben.

The haul he had acquired from the three adjacent houses had been truly impressive, minus the one disturbing find he had encountered.

Ben pulled up in front of the house, stepping out and grabbing his baseball bat. The Rolling Stones played lightly in the background from the truck stereo. "Good morning," Eve chirped from Ben's wrist, seeing his elevated heart rate.

Ben let out a sigh. "Good morning."

"It's time to go to the house," Eve said, meeting with perfect timing his exit from the vehicle. The motion of multiple things aligning perfectly put him in a good mood.

"Thanks, Eve."

Similar to the previous home he had scoured, this one had a gate. It was more for decoration than security, but it would still deter the average home invader.

"Not today," Ben said under his breath, pushing the gate open and forcing a screech of unlubricated hinges.

He had never met these newer neighbors. Ben knew the Brinkman's had been older and retired, but other than that, he didn't know them or what to expect inside the house.

Walking up the drive, he noticed the landscape had taken over a good portion of the front. Ben would come back and fix this in the near future. The back of the house was mostly dock and patio, as he knew from the slight view he had of the back of every house as he performed his morning ritual.

The door was solid, a tap of his bat confirming it was metal. He tried turning the handle; nothing. Locked. "Shit," Ben said under his breath before remembering Old People 101.

Bending over, he lifted the small flowerpot, exposing a rusted door key. "Predictable," Ben chuffed.

The lock was high-end and still plenty lubricated to accept the key and open without much fuss. He was in. The immediate rush of air lightly moved his hair. Unlike his house, after taking a few initial steps in and flicking the switch, the lights remained off.

An odd smell lingered in the air. In Ben's mind, other people's homes often smelled funky. This was different...rotten. A pet, maybe? Ben thought, gripping the bat in his hands.

Standing in the entryway and looking around, the home appeared to be smaller and more modest than the others on the cove with just two stories and a smaller two-car garage.

As he suspected, the furniture was older and mostly brown, and it was covered in either plastic or some type of knitted blanket. Ben paused, looking at the family photos next to the entrance. One could always tell they were in a home, not a house, when they were greeted this way.

Ben's contemplation didn't last long as a tapping noise echoed throughout the still house. The weather was calm and warm, making any sounds stand out.

Again, Ben gripped the bat tighter, forcing Eve to chirp to life. "Keep it up. You're burning calories," echoed throughout the vacant house.

Ben's shoulders reached his ears as tension swept over his body. He fully turned off Eve, this time reminding himself to have a stern talk with her when they got back.

Tic, scrape, tic, scrape, sounded two more times. It wasn't mechanical or sequential, which meant it was either an animal or...well, in Ben's sheltered mind...an animal.

Ben tilted his head slightly, trying to place the noise. Again it echoed. Tic, scrape, tic, scrape. He concluded something was alive. Ben reached into his holster, checking for his pistol. He took the safety off, readying the killing machine.

The house had an open plan first floor with a separate garage attached by a long dark hallway. Ben figured the sound was coming from that direction. Taking a few more steps into the space, the hairs on his neck stood on end.

He was not scared but anxious. What if someone was still there, hiding? Or better yet, what if they had a pet dog? Ben had often thought about finding a pet, as Eve could often be very one-sided.

He took stock of his surroundings, not seeing anything of interest in the open space. Ben turned on the headlamp he was wearing, beaming it down the dark hall.

Rooms shot off from the corridor; one doorway looked like a second set of stairs leading up to the second floor. Another door was tucked neatly in the middle of the hallway, and the last one was at the end of the corridor, leading to the garage.

Ben recognized the design from the model homes for the subdivision. As any house of this caliber, it had a storm/panic room installed.

The second door on the left going under the stairs was one such room and option. Ben was so focused on the noise that his sense of smell had to remind him that the putrid stench was getting worse.

Then a thought crossed his mind. What if one of the owners was held up and stuck in that room, still alive and needing help? Without thought, Ben lurched forward, putting his feet in motion.

The military-style vest he was wearing made a clicking sound as he moved. At the end of the hall, a light filled the void from a window beside the garage door. He focused on that and the light from his headlamp.

The sound took on a more frantic cadence. Tic-scrape-tic. As Ben's heart started to race, he was glad he had turned Eve off. At this point, she would be reminding him to take a shower or something.

Passing the stairs, Ben grabbed the handle of the second door. If memory served him right, the panic room would be behind another entrance tucked under the stairs, cast in concrete with a reinforced door.

Sarah and Ben had opted for the two-story version, made of filled CMU. A ladder led from their master bedroom to a mudroom downstairs, connecting the two spaces.

The first door opened with no protest at all, and it was obvious that the smell from earlier was emanating from this room. It made Ben gasp. He made a mental note to remind himself to bring a mask next time he was out.

Flashing his light around the space, Ben discerned that this was the panic room storage area. A large shelf had been knocked over in front of the panic room door, and canned rations covered the floor. The area was completely disheveled.

This must have been what had locked the occupants inside. Ben took stock of the rations and noted that they were not as nice as the ones he had back home, but they would do if ever needed.

The noise started getting louder. "Hey, anyone in there?" Ben asked without getting too loud.

No response. The ticking had also stopped.

"Listen, I'm not here to hurt you. If you've been in there a long time, I know you're probably a little confused. The door is blocked by a shelf. I'm going to move it and then open the door."

A light thump was heard in reply. That was all Ben needed to put his hands into motion.

Grabbing the shelf, he lurched the large metal contraption on its side. Cans clacked onto the floor and a few popped open. It sounded like a light car crash, and the echoing sound in the small space did not help.

However, Ben was focused, and the noise was more of an afterthought.

After a minute of maneuvering, the door was clear.

He reached down and turned the handle lightly as the door latch gave way with a click. It was unlocked. Mrs. or Mr. — or hell, both — had been in this room and gotten blocked in.

"Hey, I'm opening the door." Silence. Ben gently pushed the door as a second wave of nauseating, putrid air blew out of the room, making him exhale the air in his lungs.

It was disorienting, pushing Ben back several steps as the door opened inward into the dark void. Ben had yet to look up and was catching his breath as he fell over backward and landed on the shelf he had just moved with a crash.

Staring at the ceiling, Ben finally took a breath as a thump and drag came from the dark room. Ben had dropped his bat, and with a sudden realization of where he was, looked up into the dark void, his flashlight exposing what had been making the noise.

Ben had been right about one thing; the inhabitants of the house — well, at least one — had been trapped in that room. What he had been wrong about was them being alive.

The creature let out a moan. That was about all it could do, seeing as Mrs. Brinkman's jaw was missing and there was purple sludge oozing from her gaping hole.

The sight shook Ben to his core as he froze in place. He had, after all, never seen one of the crazies before…the zombies. Tucked away in his little castle of fortitude, Ben had been sheltered from the realities of what was happening outside his walls.

"Shit, shit, shit…" Ben trailed off. His body was finally sending signals to his limbs to get his ass moving.

The bat was behind him, as it had been the first thing to go when he had tripped. The zombie was moving slowly. One of its feet was gone, and it walked on a nub; the other foot was still in a slipper. Her fingers were what horrified Ben the most, though: All ten fingers were stripped to the bone, the gray flesh peeled back from the pointing fingers. Ben looked down and saw claw marks from months of digging, but for what? Him?

The creature was moving slowly enough for Ben to take in all the visceral details.

Six feet. Five feet. The zombie was getting closer as Ben reached for his Glock. On instinct and due to the closer range, Ben aimed and fired two rounds directly into the creature's skull. Purple gore splattered the wall behind Mrs. Brinkman.

Ben's heart was racing as he fired another round for good measure. The news reports, as well as every piece of zombie fiction, detailed trauma to the head as the fastest way to take one of these creatures down.

"They got that shit right," Ben said, standing up, wiping the spatter of gray matter from his forehead. He looked down, taking in the sight, smell, and total vision of the horror.

The contents of his stomach decided to join the party as he lurched violently, puking his guts out on the floor and adding to the disgusting chaos.

She had been alive when she had entered the room, from what Ben could tell. He turned to leave and picked his bat up with a newfound respect for the weapon. It would not be dropped so easily next time. The ringing in his ears would prove to be a distraction.

As Ben was closing both doors in an attempt to hide the horrific scene, he discovered a note he hadn't noticed earlier written into the door. It simply read, "Sorry. Do not open."

Some bastard had done this. Ben almost felt a tinge of guilt. Maybe if he had looked earlier, he could have saved her.

Then logic kicked in. Someone had put her in there because she was infected. The word danced in Ben's mind. He would decontaminate himself as soon as he returned to the house. He wouldn't even drive to avoid exposing the truck.

Ben had set up an outside shower and burn pit for such an occasion. But first, he wanted to see what was in the garage before he left. He would not be coming back to this mausoleum unless he had to.

He left Eve off for fear of not hearing anything else. He would be more careful from now on.

He turned toward the garage door. It wasn't but twenty more feet down the hall. Ben took a few more minutes to pull himself together. His ears still rang from the gunshot in the closed space, and it would be a while before that went away.

The door to the garage was clearly visible due to the window at the end of the hall. He was betting there would be no more issues, or at least, he was hoping. He had never shot anyone before. He would reflect on this and drown the memory later in whiskey.

The garage was as large as his, he realized after opening the door. The room was dark and full at the same time, with objects casting shadows at odd angles. Ben walked over to the larger, paneled doors and manually unhooked the garage door opener with the hanging string, pulling the entrance open and flooding the space with light.

Ben's jaw dropped. The garage was full of tools, large maps on the back wall, and most importantly to Ben, a base station full of long-range two-way radios.

It was clear the man had retired from the railroad. An odd bike with four spread-out track wheels sat in the back corner, surrounded by cases of what looked to be security gear.

What truly caught Ben's eye was the large map of Jacksonville on the wall. It was detailed, and it specifically laid out all the railroad tracks in and out of the cities. Red areas marked small side roads that weren't on the maps he had, including the digital one.

On the table was a booklet bearing the owner's name and prior job title. Department of energy, railroad security team. Jack Brinkman. The guy was a retired security officer for the railroad, and at some point, the Department of Energy. He remembered watching a show about people doing this line of work. They would secure important and often delicate cargo.

Sorry about the head, Mrs. Brinkman, Ben thought to himself.

Underneath the radios lay a duffel bag full of ammunition but no weapons. It puzzled Ben why the owner hadn't taken it. Something didn't feel right about the scene. The map and radio, however, lent Ben an idea.

Sarah had once said the railway was the best path to follow if the roads were ever clogged.

Looking on top of the shelf, Ben found several more maps, each for different states. These maps were like gold to Ben. He had spent countless nights thinking about Sarah's path back home, and had always landed on her following the coast. It was simple and easy to skirt around major cities.

Ben looked at the wording in the radio base and read it out loud. "Long-range signal booster." He kept his voice low, the gears churning in his head.

The events of the past thirty minutes had been more than what he had experienced in several months. The maps, radio, ammunition, and rail bike would all go back with Ben after he got cleaned up. Tomorrow would be a new day.

Ben still didn't understand all the thoughts going through his head, but he knew somewhere in the back of his mind a plan was forming. Maybe some vodka would help, Ben thought, shutting the garage door and heading to the house to get cleaned up.

With the click of a button, Eve came to life. "Hi, Ben. You have completed 2,456 steps since…"

"Thanks. Set an alarm for six a.m. Label it 'game time.' Also, mark any files on the computer regarding railroads."

The survival package had also included twenty terabytes full of what the company considered "useful data." It was like an encyclopedia, and while it did not have all the content that the Internet used to contain, it was close enough and should include information about the railroads.

"Sure thing. Enjoy your walk," Eve said as Ben took a cleansing breath of fresh air while stepping off the cement stoop.

CHAPTER 3

The alarm calmly reminded Ben it was time to wake up to the sound of an old Beatles song. "Golden Slumbers" filled the morning air, not enough to carry far but enough to fill the room.

Stretching, Ben realized he had, in fact, drank too much before going to sleep, drinking away the vision of Mrs. Brinkman.

Now that he was awake, a new thought consumed him as his feet hit the floor. Maps. The radios. Sarah.

Chugging a cup of water sitting on the nightstand, Ben realized it was full of vodka and spit it out.

"Good morning, Ben. Your coffee is ready," Eve chirped as the coffee maker on his dresser started pouring. At night, power was distributed to only a few systems, and Ben's alarms helped to manage that.

The smell of rich coffee filled the air as a fleeting vision of spattered gore quickly left his mind.

"Morning, Eve. Big day today. I think I'm going to go out soon."

"Hmm…I don't have a response for that, but I'm sure you will enjoy it," Eve chirped back.

After a few more minutes of getting himself together, Ben slogged to the shower. No morning stroll to the dock today.

The shower was another of the things he had timed. Ten minutes on low pressure; that was all the hot water he had per session. Eve would remind him during the last two minutes that his time was about up.

Standing in the glass enclosure, Ben leaned his head against the tiled back wall. After running into one of those crazies, he was starting to worry about his wife and if she would in fact, make it back through the millions obviously out there. He shook his head, dispelling that thought.

A simple plan was forming in his head. Sarah would more than likely be coming via the railroad tracks or bridges to get across the river. Ben would take a fully charged radio and note to each bridge within reason.

By his count, that would be four. He had more than enough radios now. He would also put dates and instructions on when to turn them on and the proper channel.

It was a simple plan, and even though it wasn't doing much, it was doing something. Ben would also leave notes at the house just in case.

He started humming the theme to The A-Team, thinking of the preparations he would need to make.

After what had happened yesterday, Ben had realized that he was going to have to leave the confines of his castle. Something had changed in him after the incident. He needed to see what was happening. After all, he wasn't so sure after his run-in with the zombie about the calculations he had made.

He also decided then and there to no longer tie their former names to the creatures. That hadn't been Mrs. Brinkman. It had been a zombie. She had not been human anymore. She had been something else, and he had to get his mind wrapped around that fact in order to prepare himself for what he might encounter outside these walls.

"By boat?" Ben asked himself. "No, I need to see this shit for myself, and I'm sure Sarah doesn't have a boat, I think," he concluded, talking to himself in an assured yet hungover tone.

"Two minutes," Eve warned.

Another thought crossed Ben's mind. The radios had a signal booster for FM communication. Maybe he could pick up someone else's signal.

For the past eight months, he had only been able to hear FM radio static on his stereo. Before that, it had all been easy listening music from one last radio station still playing music, which had since been silenced.

Ben would need to turn the phone on more as well and increase his communication attempts with Sarah. Again, reflecting on the dangers he now knew existed, he was determined to get out of his comfort zone.

The trip back to the Brinkman's house was simple. Ben decided to carry his flask with him, and enjoyed a few sips on the way over, calming his nerves.

Nothing had changed. The truck was still parked in the drive. He opened the garage door and began loading up the goods, including the ammunition. Ben found himself taking a few more sips during the morning tasks. "To hell with it. I say day drinking is acceptable," Ben told no one, flipping off the sky.

There were more maps than he had initially thought, and more ammunition as well. Unfortunately, Ben didn't have anything that fired a 7.62mm round, the type you used in an AK-47.

After a full day of organizing the electric-powered Toyota Tacoma and another subsequent trip for the odd railroad bike, Ben set down the maps in his dining room. The one of Tallahassee, he set on the table. The map of Jacksonville, he hung on the dining room wall where he could mark and pin it. His targets stuck out like sore thumbs.

Bridges and railroad tracks were his primary target. He would place a sign and radio in the middle of the bridges. If it was Sarah, she would know it was him. A note stating, "Stick to the plan. Ben," would be all it said.

He did worry about others finding the radios. They were his now, and he had to be sure not to let anyone know where he was. Yah, he had also watched that movie. Issue was, he hadn't heard a soul in a long, long time. He often worried if there was a reason for that. Either way, he was about to find out.

"Dinner time," Eve chirped as Ben charted out the last of his route.

Barring any unforeseen circumstances, it would take a full day and maybe even a night. He would have to be prepared. Ben would start up near the city in Jacksonville, hitting those bridges, and then work his way back home.

He would take the Toyota Tacoma, a 4x4 off-road capable vehicle. It was a smaller model and would fit better in a tight squeeze, not to mention it was at least a foot higher off the ground than his Tesla.

"Thanks, you joining me?" he asked Eve.

"Please, I need two hours to fully charge."

The two sat there in silence, Eve in her small charger while Ben stared at the map on his laptop. He was adding his route to print out and bring with him. Who would have thought they would have a printer during the zombie apocalypse?

After dinner, Ben, not following his normal routine, turned on the satellite phone. He had not turned it on other than during his morning routine for a long time.

A message pinged, making Ben's heart race again, springing Eve into motion.

"Are you OK? It's late. Maybe a little music is in order," she said as Pink Floyd's "Shine On You Crazy Diamond" came on.

"Off!"

It was a voice mail. To date, Ben had only received one text, figuring Sarah's phone was damaged. Ben took a swig of whiskey and set the phone on the table, staring at it. The message could go two ways. Everything that had happened recently had Ben on edge, and at the same time, excited.

Ben reached down, hitting the play button.

"My God, it's working. Oh God. It only works at certain times in certain places, the satellites. Ben, I got your text. The plan. I'm getting close. I'm in Florida, but it's gotten complicated. Things are—" Static.

The message clicked off. It was her. Her voice. Her amazing, buttery voice.

Eve spoke up as Ben turned her off, taking another swig from his flask.

He played the message ten more times, her voice seeping into his being. "Complicated," Ben said out loud.

She was close. He wondered what that meant. By his measure, she must have been in the Panhandle. Anything closer, he would have heard something, right?

Ben's resolve to leave his paradise solidified then and there. He would prepare tomorrow and leave the next day.

Ben returned the message and sent her a text, deciding to leave the phone on for the evening.

That night, he partied. Queen blared through the stereo as he drank his share of vodka. It was time, he was ready, and tonight, he would celebrate.

CHAPTER 4

Eve woke Ben up at 6:30 on the dot. Speckles of dull sunlight reflecting off the river filled the room. Taking a deep breath, Ben knew today was different. He had to make preparations to leave tomorrow.

He set a new routine that involved him wearing pants down to the dock for his morning coffee.

The energy-producing machine perked to life driven by Eve, the smell of roasted coffee filling the air. Ben often wondered how long that would last. He had plenty for now, though.

After brushing his teeth and putting his pistol on its holster, Ben took the walk he had completed over three hundred times. This morning was different though. He was focused on the two things he had to accomplish today.

First, he needed to pack the truck. Second, he needed to pay a visit to the admiral's house next door. There was something Ben wanted to — had to do.

The water, as usual, was calm this morning, if a little higher than normal, more than likely due to rain. As always, Ben relieved himself in the calm water, creating ripples on its surface. He sipped his coffee, focusing on the far end of the inlet opening.

A light rattle of cans caught his attention. He had strung them across the opening with a cord as an alarm, to warn him if something was coming close.

The opening had grown together more than Ben had expected, muffling the sound he was now definitely hearing. He was glad of the extra cover that had grown around this place, hiding him and his paradise even more.

Two large pulls, and the coffee was finished. Ben frowned at the change in his routine. He would have to check out the wire. "Damn animal, I bet," Ben said, waiting on Eve to reply. Nothing.

After a few minutes spent untying the fishing boat and checking to see if the electric trolling motor was still working, Ben twisted its handle, launching the cheap metal boat forward at a smooth walking pace.

He used to charge that battery every week, but had stopped some time ago as nothing ever came through the inlet. He fished from the dock when needed, but with the general lack of fishing and boats, fish were plentiful.

Pushing through some of the brush now clogging the opening, Ben saw what had set off the alarm.

Before him was a middle-aged man with an arrow in his chest sticking straight up in the air. Blood was still barely visible from the wound, which told Ben that this person or zombie had maybe been in the water no more than two days.

Close, this person was close. As he got closer, he also noticed the normal-looking skin and features, not like those on Mrs. Brinkman.

This wasn't a zombie. This was a person, and he had been shot with the arrow.

A light life vest kept the body above water. He wondered how far down the river this body had come from.

Ben pulled out the fishhook pole from the boat and poked and prodded the body to ensure it wasn't coming back to life. He was still fuzzy on how the whole thing worked with the disease. His heart was also racing with thoughts that this person may have known or been with Sarah.

He leaned over, checking the man's pockets, and to his surprise, he found a wallet.

"Port Canaveral," Ben said, shaking his head. This person wasn't coming from the same direction as her. Tucked also in his wallet was a soaking wet note. He lightly unfolded it and laid it on the metal bench seat of the boat.

It was a note to his wife. He was going out looking for her. Like Sarah, she must have been out when this craziness started.

Eve perked to life. "Would you like to listen to some calming music? Your heart rate is..." Ben again turned Eve off. Over the past three days, he had done that more than the entire past year.

Was this an omen warning Ben not to wander out? Or something more ominous? The man also had a holster; however, there was no pistol. Had he been robbed for what he had? Or even worse, been hunted? This symbolized again the threat that Sarah was being exposed to every day she was gone. It made him sick to his stomach.

After a few minutes, Ben unlocked the vest, tied a rock to the body, and watched as it sank to the bottom of the river. He didn't like the uninvited guest, and wanted to make sure that if someone came looking for him, they wouldn't look here.

Ben checked the tension on the cord of the homemade alarm and adjusted a few of the cans before he disturbed the silence of the morning air with the sound of the trolling motor, heading back toward home.

Driving back, he thought of all the things he had to do today, also worrying about how that man had ended up with an arrow in his chest at the edge of his inlet. That would have to wait until later, though. First, he had to swear himself in.

Two nights ago, while drinking, he had come up with a plan to start his own little militia, and by little, he meant a one-man army. The idea of having a sense of order and belonging calmed Ben.

It gave him a sense of normalcy, making him feel like he was in control of the chaotic world that was churning outside the walls of his gated community. The thought made him feel official in his little artificial world.

Besides, between the body-building chemicals he had been helping himself to and his lifelong experience of shooting guns and target practice, he was willing to bet that he was just as good, if not better than your average soldier. He knew as much.

On the flip side, Ben had been described by his friends as one of the nicest guys they knew, and he had often agreed with their assessment, mostly because he had left his past behind.

He was aware that he was still a nice guy,   since the fresh memories of what had happened at the Brinkmans' house were still haunting and weighing on him. Because of this, he felt that he needed a persona; one that would make people second-guess messing with him.

In theory, he could tell people he was a soldier. He did not want to get too deep into lies with anyone he met on the outside, but he had decided that if ever asked, he would omit his history. This would also help to throw people off track if ever he came into trouble.

Ben would be a pioneer in his own private army of one. Besides, he needed the confidence, and figured it would help him focus on the tasks and his upcoming experiences in a more detached and mechanical state of mind.

About a month ago, in a book he had found in the admiral's house, he had read about what it took to join the army; the swearing-in process and passing of various tests. They all seemed uncomplicated yet important. He was confident that passing a physical exam would be no problem for him, and the remaining tests could not be completed in the current situation, so it was time to jump right into the swearing-in.

Ben had decided last night that he would have Eve help him recite the oath using the flag hanging in the admiral's colonial den. Once the process was complete, Ben would be able to, in theory, say he was a soldier.

What Ben did not realize was that he already looked very intimidating, and the chance of anyone picking a fight with him was slim to none.

He paused on the walk back to the house, looking out over the water and listening for any additional signs of noise. Nothing but morning calm. Good, he thought. It was time to get packed, then he could move on to the rest of his plans for the day.

In the kitchen, Ben had laid out four days' worth of rations the night before. He couldn't think of a scenario that would keep him out longer than that.

He was taking a mountain bike in case something happened to the truck, and figured that from his farthest point, the ride wouldn't take more than a full day. The eight boxes with radios sat on the floor. He marked them in a manner Sarah would recognize.

He kept three of the radios for himself, opting to turn one on this morning to scan the channels for anything. The radio clicked to life as he hit the boosted scan button. Static and more static filled the hushed interior of the house.

Suddenly, the radio stopped scanning. There was no noise or music, just an eerie silence. "What the hell... ?" Ben whispered under his breath, taking a pull from his flask. He hadn't planned on using the radio long; he had already tested them once before, confirming they worked.

Clicking the talk button, Ben spoke in a refreshingly calm voice through the device. "Hello? Anyone in Jacksonville?"

Nothing, more static. A click reverberated at the other end. It was the sound of someone clicking a transmitter.

Ben's stomach fell to the floor. Was someone out there on the radio? Was that just a random clicking sound? He followed up again, trying to hide the curiosity and excitement in his voice. ". . . hello?" The radio went silent again. Should he hang up? Or keep talking? He voted for the latter.

"Well, if you can hear me, I'll be on this channel off and on," Ben said, confident someone had keyed up the radio. He wasn't alone.

It was apparent that the year alone had taken its toll; his heart was still racing. From what he could tell from the model numbers on the radios, they had a significant range, with the capacity to connect as far as southern Georgia.

Back in the day — well, a year ago, you would have required a permit to use one of these radios. With the booster, he believed the range was well over a hundred miles. Then again, he didn't know if that depended on several factors like radio towers or the power supplied to the booster.

He did know the handhelds could hit thirty-plus miles on a good day with flat geography. Ben sighed and placed the radios back in the boxes on the floor.

Next, Ben wrote a letter to Sarah, making copies for the boxes and, more importantly, for the house.

The letter was simple and to the point. It stated the day and month and was slightly ambiguous, not giving too much away. If she made it home, she would find the same letter. He placed them in sandwich bags to protect them from the rain and laid them on the table.

It was time to prepare for the ceremony. Ben headed to his room and put on all his "cool guy gear," as he called it, and headed over to the colonial house. He planned on using the old man's office, which had a flag hanging on the wall.

Eve had been programmed the day before with the oath, and without delay, he started the short ceremony.

Eve chirped to life, "Raise your right hand and repeat after me."

The back-and-forth only lasted a few minutes. Once complete, Ben walked over to the desk, taking the captain's rank he had found and placing it on his vest.

His plan had worked. He felt part of something and full of determination. It was his duty now to not let anyone down. In reality, Ben had always wanted to be a soldier, and was finally able to realize and fulfill that goal. Now it was time to go do some soldiering.

He didn't feel guilt, but pride. He would uphold the oath he had just taken.

Ben stopped, realizing he was talking to the empty office.

"When I get back, I may just run for president." A cool grin smoothed over his face as he took a pull from his flask, bottoming it out.

"Congratulations," Eve chirped.

It was done. He was ready mentally, physically, and spiritually.

The rest of the evening, Ben took stock of the level three rations. He was saving them for Sarah's return. These included steak and other higher-end food products.

While he was out tomorrow, Ben planned on not making many stops in an attempt to avoid exposure and to not draw attention to himself. He was, however, going to stop at two places on his way back when he was closer to home: a small grocery and a battery store close to the 295 San Pablo exit.

He figured if there was still anything in that area, he could take note. If he could get supplies when Sarah returned, they could store them and care for them as needed. However, batteries were his main concern, since they were sensitive to the heat and cold.

"Well, Eve," Ben said in a conversational tone. "We get the party started tomorrow. You need to be on your best behavior." He then proceeded to set a vibrating alarm for two hours prior to sundown and one right before noon. Other than that, Eve would just be along for the ride.

"This will be fun. Your goal for tomorrow is five thousand steps." "I'll see what I can do."

After turning off the radio and satellite phone, it was time for a few drinks to calm Ben's nerves.

He fell asleep on the couch with a half-drunk bottle of whiskey on his lap.

That night, he dreamed of meeting Sarah on one of the bridges.

CHAPTER 5

Ben stood in front of the mirror, looking at himself in a uniform he had put together and reflecting again on the events of the past three days. He had not heard Sarah's voice in months, and it had given him renewed energy.

He was ready. Taking a deep breath, Ben lightly shook his head, knowing he was as ready as he would ever be. The uniform and lonely ceremony yesterday had served their purpose. He was motivated and felt like he was part of something bigger.

The last item he checked before going downstairs was the flask in the side pouch of his light multicam body armor.

This morning had been the first time that the duo had skipped their morning ritual on the dock. Eve had even reminded him as much.

He looked at the kitchen counter, checking to make sure that the note he had written to Sarah was in place for her return. He left another where he knew she would look for the key. After his run-in with Mrs. Brinkman— Correction...the zombie, he was beginning to question his calculations as to when Sarah would return.

Ben had to keep reminding himself that that had not been a person; it had simply been a zombie that he had put three bullets into. Ben took one last moment to have breakfast before his departure. Toast,

powdered eggs, and a shot of vodka. Ahhh, the breakfast of champions.

On his way out of the house, he took measures to ensure that the house was fully secured while he was away. All the doors were locked, and the storm blinds closed, making it an actual hard task for anyone to break in. It was time.

The early morning Florida dew made everything look like glass in the light of early dawn. Ben opened the door of the truck, taking one last glance at the house before sliding into the driver's seat.

Looking forward, he chuckled at the fact that he would still have to use the windshield wipers in the morning, triggering memories of their old morning routine. Ben had always been an early riser, and Sarah, ever the procrastinator, would hit the snooze button no less than half a dozen times.

He would be downstairs and dressed for work, making coffee and catching up on the morning news, while Sarah frantically ran around the house, scrambling to find something to wear before hopping in the car.

After setting his rifle on the passenger seat, he took another calming pull from his flask. When in uniform, he would only drink vodka.

For some reason, that made sense to Ben. He enjoyed making these odd little rules lately and was even thinking about memorializing them.

He clicked Eve from his wrist and plugged her into the truck's high-end stereo system, which was managed by a large touch screen. Technology had not been shy lately, and everywhere you went, you could take your personal tech with you.

Both Eve and the truck's GPS had been preprogrammed with the route. For good measure, he had tucked into his vest pocket the paper map with his planned route.

The screen blazed to life as Eve said her hellos and reminded him to buckle his seat belt. Ben obliged. The GPS map on the truck's screen showed the path and an estimated ETA of forty-five minutes.

Ben wondered if that ETA took into consideration the apocalypse. He knew it didn't and that he would need extra time. Considering that he was leaving at 7 a.m. he should be at the Shands Bridge by three or four at the latest on his way back. That would be his last stop for the day.

Today he would not make any stops except for the ones he had planned at the grocery and battery store. The tires crunched as Ben pulled the machine outside of the property.

He stopped long enough to exit the truck and close the gate behind him. Looking back, he realized that he may want to camouflage the entry upon his return. While the dirt road and winding path covered in trees completely concealed the neighborhood, whoever had shot that arrow might be in an exploratory mood.

While the vodka had helped calm his nerves, he was shaking lightly and tapping his foot on the floorboard.

"Eve, play songs by Radiohead," he said, knowing it would calm him even as background noise.

The radio clicked to life as "Karma Police" played. Ben took another pull of his vodka.

The truck was quiet; a hybrid, as were most vehicles these days. The Toyota did not care if it was drinking gas or eating electricity from the socket; the thing would run on either.

It had been his neighbor's, the ex-athlete. Top of the line with no expense spared. It made little noise and was a good choice for this trip, given that it was dark in color and blended into the surroundings.

The unimproved road on the way to the main street was covered in brush as the wheels of the four-wheel-drive went to work. The cab bumped Ben around as he placed his hand on the rifle.

By the time Ben hit the main road, it was clear that no one had been by. He was certain, however, that he had disturbed the natural order of things as his tire tracks made it obvious someone had driven down the overgrown path.

Ben stopped out of instinct, covering the entrance to the neighborhood with brush. He inspected his work, confirming no one would notice the turnoff when passing by.

The road itself was empty. No surprise, considering he lived several miles south of Julington Creek. Grass and debris littered the road, and the tree branches would be an obstacle. He had a winch and strap if it got too bad.

The grass was peeking through the cracks in the concrete. It wasn't the most taken care of road in the county, but it was amazing how fast Mother Nature had started to reclaim her prize.

Ben clicked on the radio and satellite phone, and plugged them both up to the vehicle. He was all set.

On instinct, Ben turned the blinker on, shaking his head at the action as he pulled out.

The plan was simple. Drive north on County Road 13, through Julington Creek, and to San Jose Boulevard, then continue going straight on that road until it turned to Hendricks.

From there, he would be able to get to most of the downtown bridges in a little more than an hour. The bike would see to any roadblocks. He wasn't going to go to the far end of the bridges, figuring that would be doubling back and didn't make sense.

On this route, he would be able to scope out places to explore, and it would be easier to plan alternate routes or maneuver as needed than in the interstate. He did make a mental note to check on the highway today to see if it was clear.

Just five days ago, Ben would have never considered this plan or left the safe confines of his solar-powered, stocked home. However, his run-in with the zombie, the message from Sarah, and the dead body had changed everything. He had to do something.

Vehicles were scattered around the road, looking like small monuments. Their windows were dull and covered with a film of dirt, keeping his prying eyes out.

He crossed over the Julington Creek bridge with no issues. A few extra cars made him maneuver off the road more than he had anticipated. The crunching of debris beneath his tires from a wreck piqued his interest. One of the vehicles looked much like his neighbor's. A black BMW. He decided that he would check that out later.

It looked like the craziness had gotten close to home. Too close. Ben was starting to see the world for the first time. He had been lucky. The buildings looked as if the looting had started and stopped in rapid succession.

He supposed the crazies, before they'd turned into full-fledged zombies, had ceased any attempt to use the situation for gain. It was starting to become more apparent as he neared the stores in San Jose that making a supply run would yield results.

He had been driving for roughly forty-five minutes, slowly weaving through abandoned cars and going off the road only twice, when he reached the main shopping area. Then, it was easy for him to weave through the parking lots.

He figured there would be more obstacles once he got further down the road. "Jesus," Ben said in a hushed voice. "How did this go to shit so fast?" he asked himself.

Cars lay in random patterns; some crashed, others parked with windows caked in mold. Storefront windows — the ones still intact, were dusty and hard to see through. What struck Ben was the rapid pace in which Mother Nature had reclaimed her land. Grass sprouted from the rooftops and roads at odd intervals.

Ben looked at the clock on the dash. It was nearing 8 a.m. He had been driving slower than needed, and took that into account. He was taking in his surroundings.

In the distance, he could see the overpass. Interstate 295 stood there as an entrance gate to Ben. So far, he felt he had conquered the space up to this point. He would soon find out that he was wrong.

A ding in the GPS notified him that the battery store was on his right. It was. Several of the stores around looked to be in various stages of looting minus a handful, the battery store being one of the spared ones.

Ben chortled, "Why get batteries when you can get a new LED 80-inch TV? Stupid asses," he said under his breath. That would have been the first place he went to.

He would be back.

For the next twenty minutes, Ben slowly drove up the ramp to the I-295, wondering where all the cars were. Then he saw them. The main road had been cleared by what looked to be a bulldozer.

Vehicles had been pushed to the side like toys, making way for something. Military, Ben guessed.

He squinted his eyes, attempting to make out an unusual object to the west that he did not like. He bent over, popped the lever on his glove box, and reached for his binoculars to get a better look.

It was a wall of cars stacked up on top of each other, like the ones you saw in junkyards. The Buckman Bridge had been blocked off.

What he couldn't tell with the binoculars was if the bridge had been completely cut off. It didn't matter. He at least knew he could maneuver on the east side heading toward the beach. He would still be able to make his delivery, as far as he could tell. The bridge was not in full view.

Ben threw the truck in reverse, looked over his shoulder, and backed up all the way down the on ramp. He then turned the vehicle around and headed under the overpass toward the city. This could get interesting. City roads come with a whole different set of obstacles, he thought to himself as he reached for his flask and took another pull of vodka, calming his nerves.

CHAPTER 6

Weather in Florida was about as predictable as an old dog during the month of September: always hanging around and guaranteed to get up and make itself known at least once a day at set times. If you didn't pay it enough attention during that short burst of energy, it was liable to take a crap right there on the floor.

Ben saw the beginning droplets of rain hit his windshield as he passed the first red light after the underpass. He hadn't noticed the clouds moving in. It was common this time of year for small rainstorms to creep up. *That and hurricanes*, Ben thought.

Without the help of the weather channel, Ben used one of those sensors at the house. It didn't really tell you it was going to rain until it was pushing buckets on you.

"Great. Looks like rain, Eve," Ben said as the sky opened up, dumping rain on the slowly moving vehicle.

Ben reflected as he stopped for a minute. The rain would make it hard to see obstacles in the road, but it would also make him less noticeable just in case. He had yet to see a zombie, and it was starting to concern him a little. Maybe his neighbor had been a one-off. He hoped.

Every minute of the day felt like new baby steps. To his left, Ben saw a gas station, deciding to pull in and get out. It was pouring rain, and in the short five minutes, since it had started, it had been enough to flood the road.

The gas station had cars mainly pulled on one side in various stages of wrecks and abandonment. The convenience store stood dark, like a black void inviting guests to be lost in its depths.

Turning off the truck, Ben grabbed his rifle and jumped out of the vehicle. He would wait awhile till the rain slowed, and in the meantime, see the world the way others did now.

The rain sounded like hundreds of bullets pounding the metal roof as Ben made his way to the front door. The glass was intact, and as he tried the door, he noticed it was also locked.

"Guess there were more interesting things to loot," he said out loud, remembering several of the larger storefronts owning broken glass.

He had left Eve in the truck. He still had plenty of time, but was quickly missing the five-day forecast put out by First Coast News, his local channel of choice.

Tapping the glass, he stood back and, grabbing a flashlight from one of his many pockets, beamed the light inside. No movement. The aisles looked stocked; a few areas from his limited view looked picked over, but overall, he was surprised.

"Alright, maybe a little shopping. Snacks for the road," Ben said, having his mind dead set on a Snickers bar. He knew things were expiring but thought at least a year would be okay. After all, he remembered days of year-old Halloween candy still being good.

He would grab what he could. Not too much but enough to treat himself. Then Ben started thinking more.

"Beer. Christ, what I wouldn't do for some beers," he said, again reaching down before pulling a hammer out of the holder on his waist and smashing a small section of glass enough to open the latch on the door.

While he had plenty of liquor, beer was something he did not have. Some of the beer here would have gone bad at some point, but not all types.

The smack and crunch of glass was drowned out by the rain. Clicking the latch, Ben slowly pushed the door open, stepping over the broken safety glass that looked much like a shattered windshield, leaving small pellets of glass instead of shards.

A rush of pent-up air came through the opening as he entered.

He had come prepared this time, pulling up a light mask over his face.

It was one of the types that you pulled through your head and went around your neck; one tube of cloth that covered a good portion of your face. He used it when fishing to keep the sun off.

He had others, but this was all he needed for now. While it wouldn't completely stop the smell of anything rotting or dead, it would soften the blow.

The smell of rotted and musty food filled Ben's nostrils enough to let him know he wouldn't be finding any fresh milk today. However, he was relieved that he was not picking up the smell he had encountered at the Brinkmans' house.

The store was still in order, minus a few items that had fallen off the shelves. Bags of chips still sat there as if waiting to be inspected and chosen over their peers. Flashing his light over to the drink section, he saw that a light film was coating the glass. He could just make out that it was full.

The dairy and other cold items must have rotted, generating the moldy-looking substance. He grinned, knowing he would find beer there and maybe even a few other gems.

To his left was a hot dog machine, one of those that had the sausages laid out and rolling around till done or, as was often the case in gas stations, cooked to a dry, sweating, gross mush.

A single, oddly intact hot dog sat there.

"Damn preservatives," he uttered, shaking his head and turning around. "Bingo!" Ben grinned as the flashlight revealed a row of candy packets, including Snickers bars and what he assumed would be no good before long if not already bad, Reese's Cups.

Walking over without hesitation, Ben picked up one of the bars, slipping off his right glove. As he peeled back the wrapper, the smile on his face widened; the chocolate was still good and not molded yet.

He let out a groan of pleasure just as thunder struck in the background, forcing a bag of chips to fall.

"Damn, storm's getting nasty," Ben commented out loud to no

one, as he often did. He started to reconsider his plans.

Everything had been charted for a normal day. Rain hadn't fallen like this in over a year, and Ben had not forgotten it was hurricane season. The wind hadn't been blowing much, so Ben counted the cloud bands that had formed in the sky and landed on a nasty tropical storm.

Another boom and crash; rain pelted the roof harder.

"Okay, Okay," Ben said out loud, figuring it was some type of omen. He would go back till the storm subsided and take another go at it tomorrow.

He was still close to home and knew he had a straight path. Chewing on the candy bar, Ben decided that he would drive a few more miles to make sure the path was clear before turning back. He would at least do that much.

Looking around, he also spotted a few other items he would take. Toilet paper and some beer from the cooler.

Dropping the wrapper on the ground, Ben walked over to the cooler door. He tapped it, waiting on a response just in case. He figured he would hear something or, if there was a zombie inside, it would take a go at the door. No such movement occurred. Nothingness echoed back, drowned out by the sound of the rain.

Raising his face cover back up, Ben pulled the door open with a slow click of the handle. This time the smell was overpowering. Rotted food and whatever else had died in there.

He beamed the flashlight around the cooler to see the source. A body lay against the wall, empty beer bottles surrounding the corpse.

Ben stared at the horrific scene. Gray matter sprayed the wall behind the body, blood staining the walls. He figured it was a man based on the clothing. The body's head was bent forward, exposing most of the back of the skull.

It was gone, more than likely contributing to the mess in the wall. On his lap sat a revolver. A damn huge one, like Dirty Harry used to carry around. The name tag on his shirt read "Drew."

This body would not be fighting back. The man had gotten piss drunk and ended it. Ben stood there, thinking of reasons. Drew hadn't been cornered in the freezer or attacked. With a sigh, he settled in the man having issues.

Ben found a towel to cover the body and picked up the gun. He said a few words to make himself feel better, knowing he was just there to take some of the man's beers, then grabbed two cases of the canned beverage and left.

Closing the door of the freezer behind him, Ben put his loot by the front door, including the toilet paper and snacks. In the future, he would come clean up and put places like this as waypoints in case they were ever needed.

It still struck Ben as odd that no one had looted the obvious target.

"Guess they didn't have any big-screen TVs to steal," Ben muttered, shaking his head while looking outside.

The rain was still falling hard; however, it had settled into a steady cadence instead of the swaths that had come through at first. He would drive a few more miles, return home, then set back out the next day when the weather improved.

Picking up his first handful of goods, Ben walked around the back of his truck. Rain spattered his back, as he had pulled in just enough to get out under the awning. A dumpster sat a few feet back.

Ben didn't notice the zombie slowly lumbering toward his back in the rain as he situated his new loot. He hummed, thinking it was like finding a power-up in a video game.

The creature pitched forward. If it wasn't for the deafening pounding of rain on the awning, Ben would have already been alerted to his curious guest.

The violence was immediate. Feral, tattered gray hands lunged toward Ben as the creature's maw opened, reaching for Ben's back as he swung around, leaving the creature off balance.

It turned to follow Ben, but slipped on the wet pavement, snaking hard on the surface. Crunching bones and wet flesh added to the dance of rain.

The zombie tried to get back up before deciding to drag itself on the ground instead, not stopping or thinking. It was dressed in a suit, and the worn-through dress shoes had probably just saved Ben's ass.

There was a business park close by, and either this crazy was from there or had wondered from one of the adjacent neighborhoods. He must have been one of the last ones clinging to hope. The news, before going dark, had talked about people still trying to go about their days, not coming to grips with the situation.

Ben, realizing there may be more — not to mention the ringing in his ears from his run-in at the Brinkmans', decided on the old-fashioned way of ending the battle. He slowly strolled over to the truck, watching the creature, sizing it up.

This was his second such encounter, and he wanted to see what the thing was capable of; at least while he had his bat firmly in hand.

The crunch of the aluminum weapon on the zombie's skull was jarring, making Ben wince at both the sound and sensation the bat sent to his hands. Gore spattered the pavement and his boots.

"Shit," Ben cursed, shaking his head.

He quickly checked the body and found a wallet with a driver's license. Ben tucked it into his pocket; for what reason, he didn't know. He then dragged the body by its feet out into the rain and away from the truck. It still had weight to it. He also noticed a few other marks on its body; maybe a gunshot, and on the legs, bite marks.

A small fragment of skull crunched under his boot as he mistakenly stepped on the small piece that had shot out from the blow.

After a quick scan of the soaked area, Ben decided it was time to go. He would pay more attention next time. These things were out there.

Ben had taken well over two hours in the convenience store. The rain had trailed off lightly as he jumped back into the truck. He had pulled closer to the door, away from the spattered gore, and finished loading his cargo. Now, he was turning on the sat phone and radio.

He again heard the clicking. It sounded like Morse code. Ben had read up on it, but by no means understood it, so he grabbed one of the printed off maps and wrote the sequence down; he would check it out later. The clicking stopped as Ben replied with two of his own.

Thoughts of the creature filled his mind as he pulled out, turning back into the main road heading north. Water pooled the road, and as before, most cars had been pushed out of the road by something big.

The thing had been dead inside, its eyes gone, nothing there. Someone had once said the eyes were the windows to the soul. If that was the case, that thing had gone straight to hell at some point, and probably not by choice. There had been no person left. He knew then and there he would never hesitate or be stupid again.

A new rule was created. Always check the surrounding area first, and never go out in the rain. However, Ben would soon find this rule hard to follow.

CHAPTER 7

"**D**ammit!" Ben exclaimed as the front right tire of the truck popped, dropping the height of the vehicle a few inches and setting off alarms on the vehicle's digital readout.

Ben had been turning around in the road when something had shredded his tire. The road was still wet, and the area he had chosen to turn around in was at the mouth of a neighborhood with a large puddle of water three miles further up the road.

The trip had gone rather smooth until now, considering. Buildings closer to town had started to look more picked over. The looting was more obvious than the violence that must have occurred. Several side streets had been blocked off. Ben could only guess the reason had been to protect the neighborhoods or channel something away or into the city.

"Eve, how long do we have till sundown?"

"Five hours. Your alarm is set to go off in three."

"Well, looks like we may be here awhile," Ben said, reassuring himself but also hoping for some wisdom from Eve. It never came.

The route back to his own private castle was clear for the most part; however, due to debris and having to go around full parking lots in a few areas, it was a good hour-plus drive back.

He had been careful to avoid this. It puzzled Ben, as the tires were run-flats. He had made sure of that. Something had seriously taken a bite out of the vehicle's shoes.

Scanning the area, Ben noticed most of the buildings around were residential. He was surrounded by suburbs and middle to upper-class homes.

Ben pulled out his pistol, checking the action. Preparing to get out of the truck and look at the damage, he took a pull from his emptying flask. Another rule came to mind. Bring the bottle next time. He would soon have to check out the beer in the back.

Ben stepped out of the truck, putting Eve back on his wrist from the holder on the dash. He needed to keep an eye on the time. When you didn't have a schedule, that kind of thing could slip away from you.

Before looking at the tire, he scanned the area, remembering the lesson he had learned this morning. Rain slowly started to spatter his shoulders as he saw it dancing on the standing water.

"Great. Who in the fuck did I piss off?" Ben asked in a clipped tone.

He was starting to regret leaving home. He could have been at the back porch of the house watching the rain and sipping a margarita while listening to old Jimmy Buffet songs. He didn't even like Jimmy Buffett.

Scanning the area, he cleared the brush and walked to the other side of the road, where a fence separated the houses from the road. He would be fine from that angle.

The houses on the side where Ben had stopped sat about a hundred meters back, with a drainage ditch on either side of the turnoff.

The scene was disconcerting. He had run over a police-style spike strip. The tire was wrapped up in the spikes, explaining why the tire had been screwed like a newly married couple.

Ben just shook his head, walking over to the truck while muttering about changing the tire when a scowl crossed his face.

While he knew the truck had a spare, his heart sank. The prior owner of the truck had removed the tool kit and installed speakers under the back seat. Ben would not be going home today. He stood there, staring at the damage. He turned to look at the turnoff.

It looked as if someone had moved half the spike strip out of the way, and the section he had run over had been covered by a deep puddle from the rain. He needed to get off the street.

The houses looked like good cover, and he could look for a jack in them. Examining the spike strip, he figured he could remove it enough to slowly drive the vehicle into the tucked away houses.

He put the pistol back in its holster and got to work removing the spike strip that seemed to be designed to quickly wrap itself around the tire, stopping every so often to scan the area. After an hour, Ben was almost done.

The rain had kept up at an annoying rate. Not enough to soak you but enough to remind you it was there.

Standing up once again, Ben looked down at his wrist. "Eve, time check?" "Three hours left, and it's time for dinner. Also, the alarm to return home from your last drop is also expiring," Eve droned, reminding Ben how much

of a turn his plan had taken.

Looking back at the tire, there was one strip left that he was having trouble removing. It was wrapped around the tire in a manner that would force Ben to try and push the truck as he pulled it.

"Need a hand?" The smooth voice came from behind Ben.

He whirled around, pulling his pistol out and having it up as quickly as he turned.

Standing there in a long trench coat with a shotgun hanging off a strap and a baseball bat in his hand was a young, unassuming man.

The young man was by Ben's guess no more than twenty. Ben hadn't seen another person — other than the dead ones recently — in a year. The thought of an actual real conversation made Ben pause.

Standing roughly the same height as Ben, it was clear that while he was tall, his frame carried half the body mass. His face was innocent, wearing a toothy grin and a light beard.

His electric blue eyes held both genuine hospitality and learned caution. He was smart, and by the look on his face, had seen his fair share of chaos.

"Looks like you need a hand," the young man repeated. "Name's Ian. I watched you for a few to make sure nothing crazy was going on. I have a gun also; I could have used it," Ian said in a cool, clipped tone.

Ben lowered his pistol, finally able to formulate words. "You alone?"

Ian chuckled. "No, my partner in crime is in our safe house a few blocks back. I was making a run to the CVS. There's one tucked away on the other side of the road. Never got looted. That's why we're over here. Man, you're one scary-looking dude. You military?"

Ben was still computing the part about a real talking person. "You could say that. What did you mean when you said you were making sure I wasn't crazy?"

"Well, most people we run into are friendly. Like us, just trying to survive. Then there are a few others that aren't. Those types... well, let's just say you would have already pulled that trigger. Not all bad, just super fucking paranoid. They watched too many zombie movies back in the day. I could kill those Walking Dead writers. Everyone is more worried about people. Most are nice, like I said, but some are so paranoid."

Ben smiled, agreeing with the assessment. "I'll take that help. I just need you to pull that last strip while I move the truck. Then I need to find a jack."

"It's getting late. Best bet is to stay around here. I'll tell you what; we have a safe house, but that's ours, and it's safe because only we know about it. We used to use another house though. I'll radio my partner to meet us there. I'm sure there is a jack there, and we left supplies in that house too."

Together the two made quick work of the tire, freeing the truck from its death sentence. After sizing each other up, Ben invited Ian to jump in the truck as they gently pulled off into the adjacent neighborhood.

Ian explained that he had removed half the spike strip. He had done so on several roads. Ben was simply glad to hear another voice, and Ian was more than willing to supply conversation.

The truck slowly lurched on its broken leg off the main road, and quickly found itself under overgrown neighborhood trees.

Water pooled in many areas as the two talked, Ian pointing directions.

"So why did you move your safe house?" Ben asked, wondering about the kid's tactics — or if he was walking into a trap.

"Almost forgot," Ian said, pulling out one of those small two-way radios.

We must have been close.

Compared to the two-way radio I had, that thing was a toy. One you could purchase at a sporting goods or box store. It would carry over two miles or so, but that was it.

"Kelly, we are having a guest over. Going to Safe House One." Static filled the air while waiting on the response.

"Roger," a young female voice came over the radio, sounding possibly younger than Ian.

"All set. To answer your question, we aren't over here too often. We stay most the time close to the beach. When we do come over here, we generally go to an adjacent neighborhood, sticking to the higher-end ones.

"We came back once and noticed someone else had been through, so we moved locations. This area has generally not been fully looted, mainly due to all the crazies that got bottlenecked here due to the river. They come and go in waves. That's why I'm wondering how it is south of 295. Nobody I've ever met goes that way."

Ben reflected on that statement. He hadn't seen anything other than the zombie in the gas station.

"Zombies, they're zombies," Ben said, taking a deep breath and turning in Ian's directions. They hadn't gone far, and the truck was holding up well at the slow pace.

"Right. Anyway, whoever went through the first safe house only took some water and food, nothing else really. Just like they were passing through. We just decided it was time to shift. But don't get me wrong; we have a home base. How about you?"

Ben hesitated. The warm embrace of actual conversation had him feeling chatty, but he also knew better. The funny thing was that Ben's arms were as big around as the kid's head. If needed, Ben would be able to subdue the young man. He often forgot about it and came across as genuine. Ian was seeing this. "Yah...I have a place. I think most folks do," Ben said, keeping it simple.

"South?"

"Yup, south."

The two slowly drove up to a nice two-story house. The yard was overgrown, and only the tops of the windows on the first floor were visible through the trees that surrounded the house. Rain started to fall again.

"We're home. Looks like Kelly's already here getting the garage open." "How do you know?"

"The bikes. We usually travel by bike. I wasn't on mine due to the rain. My partner apparently brought mine over. Let's get inside. I'm fairly sure there's no one around, but meeting one new person a day is enough for me."

Ben agreed. Ian was growing on him. He reflected that if, over time, he grew to trust these two, he would let them join his little paradise. After all, there were other houses. He could even use the help getting the whole place more secure. He would see.

The garage creaked open as the two winced at the noise as Kelly walked out. She was dressed similarly to Ian but with a feminine touch. She obviously took care to present herself well, even during the end of days. Standing at five foot even, she was small compared to the two men, but looked strong. Ben was guessing she had been an athlete at some point.

Her skin was dark to the point that it was either a good tan or she was from a mixed family. Long brown hair flowed out the back of a ball cap. Brown eyes peeked at Ben as a genuine smile appeared, reaching all corners of her face.

Ben knew a genuine smile when he saw one. He figured she was either happy for the company or he was, in fact, being served for dinner.

The door closed with the same shrill, only dampened by the rain that was picking up again.

Ian jumped out, throwing Kelly a bag from his pocket.

"Thanks. Who's your new pal?" Kelly asked in a soft yet joking tone, looking at the bottle of pills.

Ben finally walked around the truck as Kelly took him in.

"Christ, think you could have found someone more intimidating? You prior military?"

"You could say that," was all Ben said, keeping his little ceremony private. Kelly shook her head and reached out her hand. "I was supposed to be. Joined a few months before this garbage kicked off. I had just finished boot camp in the navy as the evacuations started and was home for the weekend.

So, I guess I could say the same thing."

That got a chuckle out of Ben calming the group. "How's the rest of the house?" Ian asked.

"Clear, same as we left it. No one else has been inside. I did notice that big, fallen tree in the road before you turn in was moved, though. Not sure. It might have been the crazies. You know, if enough of them are together..." Kelly finished giving her update.

"Zombies. They're zombies," I said as the two looked at me.

Ian spoke first. "Yeah, we figured that out after we found a few that were nothing more than living dead meat and bones. We just haven't gotten around to saying the Z word yet. Maybe it's time."

The two snickered at an obvious inside joke. Ben had questions. These two had been out in this the whole time. He didn't want to sound stupid or as if he had been hiding when in fact, he had been sheltered. He would be smart about how he asked things.

After a few more minutes of introductions, the group quickly located a jack and even a ramp to help speed up the process. It was late; however, Ben would start working on the tire change. While he wasn't planning on traveling at night, he would be ready just in case.

"Dinner!" Kelly yelled from inside the house.

It was once again raining hard, and Ben was sure no sound was making it outside the walls. Ben hadn't pulled out his rations, but he grabbed a few beers from his truck.

The room was lit by a rechargeable lantern and candle. It was a far cry from the life he had led over the past year. His two hosts saw this on his face. "Let me guess, home's a little nicer? It's OK. So is ours, in all fairness," Ian said, setting down a plate of canned beef stew in front of Ben.

"Beers?" Ben asked, setting them on the table.

Ian smiled, gladly taking one as Kelly declined. Ben set his rifle at his feet. He had taken off his tactical vest, transferring his pistol to his waistband.

They ate in silence until they were interrupted by Eve embarrassing Ben.

"Time for dinner. Also, alarm for nightly radio check," Eve said as Ben quickly turned off the notification. He would make it up to Eve later.

The others looked at the watch. "I always wanted one of those. They cost too much, and I never got one," Ian commented as gravy dropped into his chin. He licked it off before he washed it down with the warm beer.

"Why don't you get one now? I'm sure you could find one," Ben said. "We tried. Issue isn't finding one. It's getting it set up. Now that the Internet is basically not a thing. You can't set up an account and register it, so..." Kelly trailed off, thinking of better days.

"What Kelly is trying to say is that if we had Internet for even one minute, she could get one activated and programmed," Ian finished for her.

It was clear they had tried.

"You ever thought of finding one of those things with one on and see if they have a wallet? Go to their house and see if you can get it working?" Ben asked.

"Same issue. We would still need the person's information," Kelly said. Ben would save that thought for later.

"So, what are you doing here," Ian cut to the chase, getting a look from Kelly.

Ben decided to answer while still holding his experiences of the past year in reserve.

"My wife should be back soon. I received a message from her on the phone. I'm going to check out all the bridges and leave radios and some guidance," Ben said, taking a pull from the beer. It was still drinkable, but at the beginning stages of turning.

"A satellite phone? You actually got one to work?" Ian asked excitedly.

"Sort of. It only works at certain times when both phones are on and in certain places. They're on a secured government net, so I'm guessing that's why. You know there are still working satellites. I'm just not sure why the thing doesn't work all the time. I have these too," Ben added, pulling out one of the two-way radios from the vest he had laid on the floor.

Again, Ian got excited. "Kelly, check that shit out."

"We've been looking for a long-range radio like this for...well, a long time," Kelly admitted, reaching for it.

Ben pulled it back, wanting answers. "Why?"

Ian spoke first. "Trying to get ahold of other people. Stuff like radios didn't last long."

Kelly interrupted, "I was here with my family, just out of boot camp. They made me check-in at the base when things went south. For the first few months, I was with a group of people. They eventually got thinned out when the push started to move those things either west of the river or into the water. There was always someone on the radio updating the group on their location. After dinner, can I look at it? It's kinda my thing."

"So, how do you two know each other?"

"Well, I was set up at the beach in my parents' summer house and was up in Ponte Vedra getting some supplies when I ran into Kelly. She was a mess," Ian said as Kelly smacked his arm, there obviously being more to the initial meeting.

"I don't think I was the mess," Kelly replied. It was clear to Ben the two were in love. Ben smiled at that, setting the two at ease further.

"The push?" Ben asked.

"You don't seem to know a lot for a soldier," Kelly said, raising an eyebrow. "Ian and I hadn't met yet, but we were both here when it started. I was helping while Ian was...what was it that you were doing?"

The two chuckled at another inside joke, looking at me to respond.

Ben would tell the truth, at least to a point. "I never came north of 295. Plus, I'm kind of new to the soldier thing." He would leave it at that. If things worked out, he would tell them the truth. He may even get them to join, further bringing some kind of organization to the world.

The three just looked at each other, not taking the conversation further. Ben liked the air of mystery around himself but also truly needed something to hold onto. The ceremony he had held prior to going out into the wild had given him the push he needed.

"So, what was left of law enforcement and the military figured that if they could clear the zombies out of the area between the Intracoastal and the St. Johns, there may be a chance to regroup and set up a base. After NAS JAX burned to the ground, people were forced to do a lot of things. I'm sure you at least know all communications went down. That's why the radio is probably more helpful than anything. I know a bunch of those folks had to survive. Plus, we find stuff all the time. I bet there are hundreds of people around; they're just tucked away like us." Ian took a break, taking a pull from the beer. He wasn't a drinker, and his face made that clear.

"So, what went wrong?"

Kelly finished what Ian had started, obviously being more involved in the operation. "The damn things south of I-295 went wrong. A flood of them came like a vacuum cleaner and just swallowed the whole thing up. It came out of nowhere. Some asshole who said he was from that area alleged it was clear, so there wasn't as much security that way. Kept talking about his nice waterfront house and his BMW. Gave everyone the creeps. I never met him, just heard about him.

"The interstate was a perfect line of defense as we just had to stack cars on the sides. It took weeks, but we got most of it done. Then bam, we wake up one morning, and thousands of crazies are overrunning our camp. I'm guessing you came up San Marco. That is the one area we hadn't barricaded yet for at least two miles in either direction." Kelly paused, reliving the unpleasant event in her mind's eye.

"Jesus," Ben said, staring at the girl.

She took a deep breath. "It was over in less than a day. Some of us took shelter and made it through the night only to wake up and find them gone—almost all of them. Like something was drawing them back south of the interstate. We've thought about it many times. Maybe radio waves or radiation or a bigger meal, who knows. We figure it's something."

Ben sat there in contemplation. He hadn't even heard the shuffling of feet. That told him it wasn't anything around him. "You guys know of anything in that area?"

"We've been thinking about that. Thing is, once south, they can just slip over to I-95 and go all the way to Miami," Ian said before standing up and picking up everyone's trays.

"What about the bridges?" Ben asked, needing this piece of information. "Most of them were either bombed or barricaded. The only two I can think that are still standing are the train bridge downtown, and you can still get through one side of the Buckman," Ian informed.

Ben reflected on this news. That meant the Shands Bridge was out, further complicating things. He would figure out a way to address it. Reason dictated that there was a 99 percent chance she would try to use the Shands Bridge.

It didn't matter. He had heard her voice. She was alive and on her way. If the satellite phone hadn't cut off, he would have known where and gone to her. Kelly continued talking as Ben zoned out, not hearing what she was saying.

". . . you know," Kelly finished as Ben snapped out of it.

"Yah, sure," Ben said, realizing that a year without human contact had changed him. Instead of spilling his guts, he was being more selective about what he said. He would talk to Eve later. Ben was feeling guilty for leaving her out of the conversation.

Kelly and Ian, on the other hand, had been talking to others up until recently. The past several months it had just been the two of them, and they were more than happy to talk and talk, especially as Ben was keen to listen.

"Tell you two what," Ben started, sniffling lightly after a day of being soaked in the rain. "I'll tell you my plans for the next couple of days. By the sound of it, I could use the help, and you two know your way around. Things work out when I head back to home base, I'll consider bringing you two along."

The room was quiet for a minute as silence hung in the air.

"Really? We weren't going to ask, but I mean, you show up here in a practically brand-new top-of-the-line truck that works. Everything you have is super nice and not worn. You look like you could rip a building full of crazies apart. I'm not asking any more about your background, but it's clear wherever you came from is better than most of everything we've seen," Ian said while shaking his head in affirmation.

In reality, Ian had been getting medicine for Kelly as their stores had ran out. While they had a house on the beach to call home, things like power and food had become an issue. One they were desperately trying to solve.

They had traveled over thirty miles to come here, and Ben knew it. He had plenty of food and electricity to spare. The help would be worth the extra drain. Plus, people, real people. They could even fish, which was one food source that Ben hadn't taken much advantage of due to his stores of food.

The three talked for another hour about the events that had taken place before Ben headed off to the garage to work on the truck, promising to turn on the radio in the morning, even considering giving them one.

CHAPTER 8

Ben awoke with a start, startled by Ian tapping on the glass of the truck. He had fallen asleep on the passenger seat after fixing the tire. The garage door was closed, and he was safe.

His stomach rumbled from what he guessed was the old beer, making the cab smell less than appetizing as he opened the door. Ian immediately put a finger to his mouth, a stressed expression on his face.

He slowly climbed out as Ian walked up beside him. Ben was not fully awake yet, and for some reason, he reached for his pistol. He had kept it close during the night just in case the two were playing him.

Ian shook his head, pointing at the gun and snapping Ben out of it.

Ian could have gotten Ben if he had wanted to while he slept. Why wake him up? Ben rationalized, shaking it off. Ian pointed up and signaled for Ben to follow him.

Ben did so, the droning patter of rain silent for the first time since the previous morning.

They walked upstairs as Kelly stood in the hallway with a rifle similar to Ben's. These two weren't as defenseless as Ben had thought, and he didn't blame them for not showing him all their cards.

The trio walked down the front hall, Ian moving slowly as to not make noise. The hall was long and dark. Pictures of a happy childhood adorned the walls. While interested in the lives of the prior occupants, he would save that for another day.

As they turned into the front bedroom overlooking the street, an odd shuffling noise started to catch in Ben's ears. Ian reached into a backpack sitting by the window, pulling out a pair of what looked to be some cheap, knockoff night vision goggles, and pointed outside.

Ben let out a dry gasp as the weight of what he was looking at landed on him like a bowling ball through a windshield.

Zombies, hundreds of them. They were moving in some odd cadence down the street toward the river, all going in the same direction.

Ben looked over, about to speak, but this time Kelly held up her finger in a sign of silence. The lack of rain reinforced the fact that the noise would not be masked.

The three of them slowly made their way back into the hall and into the master bedroom, entering the closet. It was enclosed on all sides by walls, so it was safe to talk and turn on a light in the sealed space, shielded from the exterior.

"What the hell?" Ben asked as Ian turned on an LED Coleman's camping lantern. The light was overly bright and blueish, making Ben squint.

"That's one of the biggest masses of those things I've seen in a while. This is what we were talking about. They get all clumped together like a school of fish and keep making this circle," Ian started, being cut off by Kelly.

"They always do the same thing. They walk all the way to the river then turn south. We think there are a few different groups. Some we know left. The one we are tracking always seems to stay around here. You may not be going back that way for a few days. Plus, they pick up stragglers and leave others behind. It's the oddest thing. Like they are playing ping-pong between the intracoastal and the river. I would think they would go south and keep going, but they don't."

"There are hundreds," Ben said, scratching his light beard.

"Probably thousands if it's the same group we've been tracking. We didn't think they would be here yet. That's why we came from town and followed the river down. We estimated they would be around Avenues Mall. The weather may have flushed them out of where they were," Kelly said, taking a breath.

"SPH," Ben said, grinning at the two giving him puzzled looks. "Shuffles per hour."

The two cracked a smile, snickering as Ben started to giggle while trying not to let out a laugh. They continued that way for several minutes.

The three spent the night in the closet just to be safe. The next morning, they awoke to find the streets mostly empty. As the two had stated, a few zombies lingered in the road, lost and just staring up at the sun. It looked as if they were soaking in the warmth, drying out their rain-soaked bodies.

As if the gods knew it was time to start the party, thunder rolled in the background. Ben went down to the truck and picked up Eve, clicking her on. Eve let him know she was not happy by the flurry of alarms and daily routine notes. He decided to leave her on while in the house.

"It's alright. We'll play some Talking Heads on the way home, promise," Ben said, looking down at the watch and seeing the alarm to check the radios that he had projected would be set up.

"It's time for breakfast. I'll remind you later today that you are to turn on the sat phone at 5 p.m." Eve said as a final reminder that they were a team.

Ben grabbed one of the two-way radios and then walked back into the adjoining kitchen. Kelly was making coffee.

"Where's Ian?" Ben asked as Kelly set down a cup in front of him. "He's clearing the yard before it rains. It will give us some extra breathing room just in case."

"You guys have this down."

"Yup. So, it's pretty obvious that while you look the part, you weren't in the military. I wasn't going to say anything, but I get it. You damn sure look like it, though. I would keep that up. You never know. We've ran into some odd people. Ian trusts you enough to leave you alone with me, so..." Kelly said, sitting down.

Ben was sure she could handle herself, but the affirmation was appreciated. "How'd you know? I mean, I just want to do the right thing. Make something new."

"Two things. For starters, military people always talk about what unit they were in and what they did. And second, the group I was with was doing the same thing. Some of us had gone through training. Others hadn't. We still did the whole ceremony."

Ben chuckled, letting some coffee dribble down his chin.

"Oh, you did the same thing. It just means that we are on the same page. Look, we need your help. We live in this crazy paradise of a house on the beach. Issue is, it wasn't really prepared for this. Hell, nothing and no one was. You, on the other hand, you look prepared. I wouldn't doubt that you've been holed up somewhere. I even bet this is your first time out. We can make it on our own, but we're trying to think more long-term."

It was clear that Kelly was fishing for information. Ben just grunted, sipping his coffee.

She knew the type, mysterious and brooding, but Ben was different. It was like he was seeing the new world for the first time. She and Ian had decided in private to do whatever they could to team up with Ben.

The rain started pouring again as Ian walked in. "Hey, honey, I'm home." "Perfect timing. Coffee's hot, and Ben brought in a radio," Kelly told him, pointing at the fresh pot. She had made it on a small propane camping stove.

"How many of them did you clear out?" Ben asked.

"Five. That includes the two out in the road. I don't think there will be too many more after this rain; they'll just keep moving. These ones were pretty worn-out; I don't think they would have gotten much further. We started seeing that two months ago. The ones that turned at the beginning are starting to fall apart. Wearing their feet out, then crawling till there's not much left to move. By the way, the rain is coming in from the northwest," Ian said as all three of them groaned.

That meant one of two things. Either a tropical storm was coming in or a possible hurricane. Ben, while thinking about the weather, hadn't thought of the effects it could have on his humble abode.

"I don't think heading south for a few days is a good option," Kelly said, winking at Ian, receiving a toothy grin from the young man.

"True. I'll take your word for it. You guys came from downtown?" Ben asked, formulating his day's plan and figuring staying out here would be his best option. He could think of nothing more than a warm shower, a cold cocktail, and watching reruns of The Walking Dead, but that would have to wait.

"Sure did. Things looked clear. Not sure how your plan with the bridges is going to work out, though. They are pretty messed up, no chance there. The train bridge is probably your best bet. They bombed the hell out of the whole West side of the city. If you get across, you could take a bike and backpack and probably hit the other two main bridges from the other side. I wouldn't go much further than the stadium; we haven't been north of there, so we're not sure if it's safe or not," Ian said, making sense.

"Look," Kelly spoke, reaching out for the radio Ben had just placed on the desk. "I don't think you should leave these out there. Maybe one or two, but these things are valuable. I don't think they would stay there long. Maybe just leave the signs and a note pointing toward the one on the rail bridge. I'm pretty sure it gets used, but you can leave a clue. Something only you two would know about?"

Ben thought for a minute, not taking long before coming up with the perfect idea. He had seen a couple large teddy bears upstairs, not too big but big enough to be noticed if someone was looking for it. He would leave a note at the other bridges to look for the first thing he had given her on a date.

On their first date, Ben had won Sarah a teddy bear. He would put the radio along with a note in the stuffed beast.

"I'll go after we eat. I'm not waiting around longer than necessary. I still have a few stops to make on the way back as well. You guys cool if I stay here again tonight?" Ben asked, emptying his cup.

"Sure. I'll do you one better; we'll go with you downtown.

The rain may make it hard to navigate, but it will also cover our movements and the truck. Like Kelly said, I wouldn't head south for another day. Should be clear by then at the speed those crazies were moving," Ian said, standing up.

The rain started pounding harder on the windows as the wind picked up. It wasn't the best conditions to go on a field trip, but Ben would not wait any longer. He even considered just leaving the two behind.

"All right. Tell you what; pack enough things for the afternoon, and when we're done, we'll come back here for the night. Then, if things work out, you guys can head south with me," Ben told them as he scratched his light beard, looking at the two.

Smiles erupted from Ian and Kelly. The pair was along for the ride and weren't going to let Ben down.

"Here you go," Ben said as he slid the radio over to Kelly.

Kelly's knowledge of the device was apparent. She picked up the radio, handling it as if it were an extension of her. After clicking a few buttons and turning some knobs, the static turned into a light voice that was barely audible. Kelly concentrated on the black radio in front of her. With a few more twists of the knobs and a couple more clicks of the buttons, a voice came loud
and clear over the radio.

"Three, Zero, Zero, A, Philip, Randolph."

The radio repeated itself another five times as the group sat listening in silence. It was obviously a recorded message. Ian had a pen and paper out, taking notes.

"What does it mean?" Ben asked, again figuring they knew more than he did about the outside world.

"It's a recorded message from the people I used to travel with," Kelly said, raising an eyebrow and looking at the others. "This is an old message. I bet it's been playing for a while, but the plan was that if anyone was at a secure location, they would send the address out in a way that only we would know how to put together. It's the Veterans Arena."

The smell of rain started filling the room as water started to puddle in the yard. A small drip, drip could also be heard from a

59

leak somewhere in the roof of the house.

"That's not too far from where we're going to be today. I'm not sure this weather is the time to check it out, but if everything works out today, maybe we can stop by to see if anyone's there," Ben told them, seeing approval in the faces of his two new companions.

"We'll pack a bag. Enough for the day and night, just in case," Ian said, standing up.

Ben was starting to worry about the weather. It hadn't rained this much since the current shit show had started. He made his mind up then and there that he would head back to his Fortress of Solitude no matter what the next morning.

After an hour of clicking and shuffling gear, the trio was ready. Ian and Kelly had in fact, been through the area right up to the bridges, staying on the east side.

The two were smart and always kept the river to their side, keeping it as an escape route if needed. They carried three small inflatable life vests still sealed in bags. One for each of them and another one to throw their packs and weapons on to float across the river.

Ian and Kelly traveled light, riding bikes. The fact that they had all this stuff in what was their second safe house convinced Ben the other one must be loaded. It was a good idea, and one he would use if he ever decided to venture back out after the mess he had witnessed.

With all their gear ready, they put their things into the truck. The four-door Toyota had plenty of room, and Ben had moved some of his gear out of the covered back, making room for the bikes.

He regrettably had to leave some of the beer behind. He marked the house's location on his GPS and map with their permission. He would stop by later to retrieve the goods he was leaving.

Like clockwork, Ben started his routine of prechecks. "   Eve."

"Hello, Ben. You have several time alarms set for today labeled 'clean up.'" "Eve, change of plans. Cancel them. Set new alarms," Ben started, going on to set a handful of reminders to keep their trip on track.

Ian and Kelly were both impressed with his organization and actual ability to use what he had, as most computers and gadgets were nothing more than paperweights now — that is, if anyone gave a shit about paper anymore.

Except toilet paper. Ben had learned this from one of his favorite zombie series, one he had read repeatedly. The lesson was clear to Ben. Grab the fluffy white stuff when you find it.

With the route approved by Ian, they slowly opened the garage door and quickly realized just how much it had been raining. Two bodies that the younger man had dispatched lay in the road facedown, water coming up to their ears. "Damn," Ben said to Ian, looking up at the sky as rain misted in the air, hitting them both, the house shielding them from the main onslaught. "What?"

"Look over that treetop. See that thin band of clouds?" "Sure, what is it?" Ian again asked, his youth showing.

"Looks like the outer bands of a tropical storm or hurricane. I don't think it's going to be too bad, as it's been a solid twenty-four hours, but I bet it's going to keep raining. We need to check out the river."

Ben and Kelly jumped in the truck as they slowly pulled out. Ian closed the garage door before jumping in the passenger seat, giving Ben a thumbs-up.

The truck pulled away from the house as rain continued to remind them that the day ahead would be long. Ben looked over, seeing the zombie Ian had dispatched pushed off to the side of the road. A gentle reminder to be on the lookout.

Back on the main road after pulling out of the neighborhood, Ben asked Ian to point out any other spike strips, maneuvering around them when they came upon one.

"Is it always like this when that gaggle comes through?" Ben asked while looking south, desperately hoping his path back home would be clear.

"Most of the time. It still freaks me out. Last time we went out, we found what looked like a last stand. Bullet casings everywhere, and trucks lined up. I think it was somewhere around the mall.

My theory is that a group was holed up there and was trying to thin out the group of zombies, only to find out that it was bigger than the last time or than what they had expected," Kelly said, handing Ian, who was sitting on the front seat, a beef stick.

The spicy smell of the meat-filled the truck.

"Look, Goodbys Creek," Ian said, pointing at the bridge.

Ben remembered this spot. They used to take their friends' boat and go to the Hooters every so often. Luckily, the bridge was still intact. In fact, Ben was thinking of setting up a radio and note there. He would wait to see how the rest of the day played out first.

"Anyone want some wings?" Ben chuckled, then stopped the truck as he saw the three-story-high boat storage, full and seemingly untouched.

"I was going to ask you, why not use a boat?" Ian spoke as Ben pulled around an abandoned car and stopped by the side of the road to think.

"Didn't want to get stuck by myself. Plus, I don't think she would be coming by boat. It just wouldn't make any sense. When Sarah gets here, I'm planning on doing just that though. The boat storage by Julington Creek was mostly burned down when I passed it. I have access to a boat but was thinking about finding one a little different," Ben responded, scratching his beard in thought. The sight of the boats had taken the men's attention off the waterline, which was rising.

"Look at the water," Kelly reminded the two. She couldn't figure out if they were reminiscing about days long since passed, when you could buy greasy chicken wings from scantily clad women, or the boats. She figured both, letting out a sigh.

Kelly was right. The water was up by at least two feet, according to the marker. That would affect inlets and creeks. A bead of sweat formed on Ben's forehead.

"Sounds like someone's staying by the water," Ian said, figuring it out.

Ben reached down, pulling out his flask and taking a pull. The other two looked at him.

"What? It calms the nerves. Plus, the way I see it, day drinking is acceptable now," Ben defended himself as Kelly and Ian started laughing. It was enough to fog the windows. Ben shook his head as he pulled out slowly and continued driving.

"Eve, mark the map as green here with a boat icon."

"Sure thing. Would you like to listen to any music?" Eve teased Ben. "No."

Ben was starting to get self-conscious about his interactions with Eve in front of his newly found friends.

"There are two more bridges before we hit the Fuller Warren, Acosta, and Main Street bridges. You want to head toward the Acosta. Also, with all this rain, you may want to stay on the main road when it splits to Hendricks Avenue," Ian said, chewing his lip, genuinely thinking of the best route.

"Yeah, I'm with you. Plus, San Jose gets a little tight back in the neighborhoods," Ben agreed, glad he actually had a sounding board to reason with.

The road a quarter-mile down was blocked, forcing Ben to traverse the curb and adjacent parking lot once again. They had been driving for a little over an hour. Traveling as slow as they were due to the abandoned vehicles put them close to the targeted times Ben had projected.

The rain, on the other hand, was another story.

CHAPTER 9

The trio pulled up to the railroad tracks, pulling alongside the adjacent hospital's parking garage and pushing further around other vehicles till they got to the large apartment complex by the water. They could go all the way up to the tracks from there.

"Dammit," Ben said. Just as he thought they had a clear shot to the bridge, water was covering the far end of the parking lot, forcing him to look back at the parking garage. "Change of plans. We're going to the garage."

Ian and Kelly looked at each other, obviously not happy with the change. "Hey, man, I understand you want to get this over with, but that garage probably isn't going to be the safest place," Ian informed, looking back at Kelly as she pulled her rifle closer to her chest.

The team was loaded with plenty of ammunition and guns, at least Ben thought so.

"I know we haven't seen many zombies because of the rain, but if what you said is right, I doubt many of them hang around the water's edge anyway. They must have moved on," Ben noted, making perfect sense to himself.

"Or they've taken shelter," Kelly said, grimacing. Again, Ian and Kelly looked at each other. They must've come to a decision as the two nodded at each other, sitting up straighter.

"I'm just going to pull up the first ramp to get a little distance between us and the ground. We're not going all the way in," Ben explained much to the approval of his companions.

He slowly maneuvered the truck around an abandoned vehicle. Its windows were smudged and looked as if they were covered with mold on the inside. He was sure there was a body in there.

The rain was still falling; however, at a lesser cadence than it had in the morning. Ben figured that it would be enough to cover up any noise they made as he slowly pushed the truck through the parking garage's entrance.

The yellow-and-black boom barrier installed to keep unwelcome guests out at one time snapped, shattering into a dozen pieces as the truck eased into the dark space. The road immediately veered upward toward the second floor. They would park at the top of the ramp and get out; no need to go further into the garage.

"All right, here's the plan. I brought three backpacks, each with a radio. I can't see the far end of the bridge due to the rain, but if what you're saying is true, once we get to the other side, I'd like to have the option to drop these off. My main worry is the train bridge getting covered in water. We need to be in and out as quickly as possible," Ben declared as he opened the door, letting the sounds of rain fill the truck.

"Kelly and I will go ahead and check out the Veterans Arena. That's where the radio message was pointing to. I don't think we'll run into any issues, and on these bikes, it'll probably take about forty-five minutes to an hour at the most," Ian mentioned as the pair walked around the back of the truck, both having M4s hanging off the front of their bodies.

It was just a little over a mile each way, and while the rain would slow them down, the two would be able to make it back in time.

Ben knew he couldn't stop the two, but he had hoped they would stay with him. "All right, here," Ben said, walking back around the truck before reaching in and grabbing one of the extra radios. "Look, let's check in with each other every fifteen minutes or so. This all works out, I promise to take you back with me in the morning."

Ian and Kelly both smiled. "That's the best thing I've heard all day," Kelly beamed, clicking the radio on and putting it inside her vest after doing a quick radio check.

They had decided on a separate channel at the high end of the radio band to avoid others using the same. On top of that, the radios were encrypted, and one could monitor more than one channel.

The sounds of the repeating signal came back on the radio. Kelly turned the volume down and reached down to pick up one of the backpacks with the radios.

"Tell you what; you leave those here. I'll take an extra one with me, and we'll worry about the other bridge whenever you get back. I have a feeling we might be in a rush to get out of here if the rain picks back up," Ben said, not wanting to give up too many of his radios just in case.

While he trusted the two, he still felt as if he needed more than a couple of days to give them more of the precious treasure he had found.

Several loud clicks came from deep inside the dark void of the parking garage, followed by the light baying of something falling. The three froze, looking at each other.

"I don't think a person did that. As long as we don't go inside the building and the rain covers our sounds and smell, we should be fine," Ben said quietly, closing the doors of the truck and locking them via Eve.

The truck didn't beep, no lights went off. The doors just locked. Ben was showing her off to his new friends.

With all their gear and the mountain bikes unloaded, the team went down the ramp and out into the rain, each splashing as they hit the open pavement. There was a light fog coming off the river. Between that and the rain, Ben couldn't make out the other side of the bridge.

"Once we get over the water, you'll be able to see what we're talking about. They literally bombed or shot a missile at every bridge except for this one. They got half the Buckman; it's still dangerous and a little messy, but stable enough to travel through," Kelly said, talking loudly to cut through the wind and rain.

The water was three feet or so below the bottom rails. Someone had lowered the bridge on the other side; Ben remembered it always being up.

Ian and Kelly pulled up beside Ben, knowing what he was about to see. Ben stopped dead in his tracks, not even twenty feet into the bridge.

"Holy shit," was all Ben could utter as the condition of the Acosta Bridge came into full view.

Rebar, concrete, and various other forms of debris reached out of the edges of the far end of the bridge. It took Ben's breath away as he sat on his bike, staring at the devastation. Whatever reason the military had had to do this, it was clear that it had been to keep something in or something out.

"It gets worse on the other side of town," Ian went on, also staring at the carnage, an expression of unpleasant memories crossing his face.

Ben sat there reflecting. How could he have missed all of this? He should have at least heard the missiles or bombs being dropped on the bridges, but he hadn't. For all Ben knew, it had been on one of the afternoons where he had been wearing headphones, working out in the house gym.

"Let's get moving," Ben urged as he pushed with his left foot, lurching the bike back into motion.

By the time they reached the other side of the bridge, the rain had started to pick back up. Ian and Kelly took off toward the Veterans Memorial Arena, heading right as Ben watched them until he could no longer see the back of their bikes.

Ben pedaled up to the small building to the right of the bridge, scanning the area to the west of the train tracks. Several large buildings sat there ominously, accepting the rain and the threat of flooding waters.

Following his plan, Ben would post a sign at the very front end of the bridge, on the first thing he could find. As luck would have it, there was a junction box right as the land dropped down into a culvert leading into the river.

There, he would place his sign referring to their first date and the teddy bear he had won her that night playing ring toss, with instructions to look inside of it.

Next, Ben would ride back to the middle of the bridge where the I-beams linked into the supports. There he would pull out the teddy bear from his bag and put it on the left side of the bridge.

Sarah was left-handed, and as anybody left-handed knew, you more often than not looked to the left. While obvious to Sarah after reading the note, you would have to understand what you were looking for.

Ben had accomplished his mission. He had set up the first radio on one of the only two bridges that spanned the mighty St. Johns River.

Looking around again, Ben felt as if he had accomplished something. Something big, something great, something that meant something to somebody, to him, to Sarah. He was doing something.

Adrenaline started pumping through Ben after completing this task. Now, he would work his way down to the Fuller Warren. This bridge was one of Ben's main targets, as it was also home to the I-95, the main causeway up and down the East Coast.

Then he would move on to the Acosta Bridge, as it was only a couple hundred feet up the tracks, and figured he could quickly hit it before leaving. In order to conserve radios, he would just leave a sign at the Acosta directing Sarah to the train tracks directly below. The Main Street Bridge may have to wait.

"Ben, over," Ian came over the radio.

"Loud and clear," Ben replied, stopping his bike right before it met the land on the railroad tracks. The smell of rotted fish, to Ben's surprise, filled the air.

"It looks like somebody else has been through here. We're by the old coffee factory, and the roads, including the sidewalks, are all blocked. We can probably go around, but I'm not sure how long it's going to take," Ian said, obviously disturbed by what he was looking at by the tone of his voice.

Ben, invigorated by the small victory of setting up a radio and sign, was feeling good. It would take him some time to set up the other radio, and it was still before one o'clock.

He also felt justified in trusting his new partners, since Ian had called him over the radio and reported in. While setting up the radio, he had almost forgotten about his two companions.

Ben pedaled toward the I-95 overpass as a gust of wind almost pushed him over. While not overbearing, the storm wasn't cutting him any slack. As he made his way to the off-ramp, Ben realized his options were slim.

The bridge was completely destroyed. What had not been demolished in the blast, had failed structurally.

Ben sat there as the rain smacked his shoulders and hood. He would just leave a sign pointing to the other bridge. People would be able to see the destruction from a distance and not give the bridge a second glance. He would not leave a radio here. No one would walk up to this.

Looking down at his watch, he realized time was indeed marching on. "Ian, you copy?" Ben said into the radio, the pounding of rain loud in his ears. Ian replied; however, Ben couldn't make it out. "Damn rain," he grumbled. Ben turned his bike around and headed back down the ramp as fast as he dared to in the wet conditions, the muzzle of his rifle smacking against the bike frame.

He pulled under the overpass, doing a quick scan and staying just out of the reach of the rain. It was dark, and the road going to the other side had been blocked by trucks and various other vehicles.

Another stand had happened here. "Can you hear me now?" Ben asked jokingly, remembering the days of cheesy cell phone commercials.

"Yup. We're almost to the arena. Kelly and I are going in on foot and turning the radio down. Just buzz us; we'll buzz back. It's a mess over here. Something happened, and recently. We haven't spent much time on this side of the bridges since they were blown out. Keep an eye out. We're just going to see if we can spot anyone then leave," Ian informed him, confirming again that the two were smart and respected his timeline. He was bringing them back with him.

Ben turned quickly, hearing a clank from the pile of heavily damaged vehicles. Bullet holes that had rusted lead Ben to believe that this whole scene had happened when the shit had initially hit the fan.

"Great," Ben muttered under his breath. He could just as easily pedal away or make sure there was one less roadblock standing in Sarah's way. That reminded him that he needed to turn on the sat phone tonight.

Ben dismounted his bike and held up his rifle, making ripples in the puddles as he slowly walked toward an overturned car, the source of the noise.

Taking a deep breath, Ben picked up a can lying on the ground and tossed it in front of the car. The noise stopped momentarily before being replaced by a groaning, hissing whine.

For some reason, Ben's nerves started to tweak, sending jolts of "we need to get the hell out of here" messages.

The zombie appeared from behind the car. Its skin was gray and blue. It had been in the rain, and from what Ben could tell, was doing the same thing he was: seeking shelter. Can the damn things think? Ben thought to himself.

The semiautomatic assault rifle that Ben carried was heavily modified; it even had a silencer on it that he had found at his neighbor's — the good admirals house.

Ben knew his way around weapons. While the silencer would muffle the shot, the rain would do the rest of the job; he wasn't trying to attract any attention.

Ben looked into the empty eyes of the gray-skinned creature that had once been a person. It had, at one time, been wearing blue jeans and some type of graphic T-shirt. A round earring hung low on a lobe that looked as if it was about to fall off the side of its head.

A rush of wind continued to vandalize Ben's senses as he got a handful of the zombie's stench. The thing was roughly twenty feet away and lumbering slowly.

It wasn't a newer zombie, but it wasn't an older one either. Ben lined up his sights, placing the red dot directly in the middle of the zombie's forehead just as it reached its arms up and lunged.

The rapid cadence of the muffled rounds echoed slightly as the shell casings dropped to the ground, quietly tinkling on the water-covered concrete.

The zombie's head exploded; gray matter sprayed the already bullet-riddled car behind it. The rest of his body flew back, forcing the creature to crumple to the ground in a violent action.

Ben stared at the body for a minute before finally shaking it off, the reality of what he had just done settling into acceptance. Not even a few seconds after he had regained his composure, more sounds started emanating from behind other vehicles.

Scraping, hissing, and groaning all came together in a chorus of bad news. He had awakened the sleeping beast.

Before Ben could discover what great treasures he had just discovered, he jumped on his bike and pedaled back out into the rain, looking over his shoulder only to make sure he wasn't being chased.

Ben would haul ass to the Main Street Bridge and then radio his newly found companions. Thoughts kept flashing through Ben's mind as he huffed, pedaling the bike as fast as he dared on the slippery roads, splashing through puddles as he went. He would pass directly by the Acosta Bridge on the way back, making that his last stop.

Visions of days long since passed, and some in the not too distant past crossed his mind. Sarah had been out on this world for a whole year while he had stayed behind his protective walls, living a life unimaginable to what he assumed was the rest of the world.

Ben's radio came to life just as he was reaching the bridge. He had been so focused on his thoughts he had almost missed the turnoff; he hadn't been downtown in quite some time.

"Hey, it's Ian, over," Ian whispered. He was obviously trying to be quiet.

The rain was still constant as Ben scrunched his face, trying to figure out why Ian would be lowering his voice.

"Go ahead," Ben replied, pulling under the front entrance of one of the buildings on Independent Drive.

"There are people here. Not sure how many. We were about to walk up to one when we realized he was walking someone tied up in chains into the back parking garage. We're heading back. By the looks of this guy, I wouldn't recommend wandering too far off," Ian whispered again in a rapid, hushed voice.

With that, Ben decided to make his second drop on the Main Street Bridge then head back to the rail bridge.

While the center of the bridge was destroyed, it still had some of the base structure left. He would leave another sign here. For some reason, he felt the urge to leave another radio.

The area was open and inviting. He could envision someone from the area walking right here, trying to get their bearings. After all, he had the sign and bear that he hadn't dropped at the Fuller Warren Bridge.

Thoughts of the man the others had reported crossed his mind. He had taken their comments on people they had run into at face value. Also, every sign of a struggle that Ben had run into during his short stint into the wilderness had been that of the struggle between man and the crazies.

The rest of Ben's journey back to the train tracks was uneventful, and he dropped his last sign at the Acosta Bridge.

Something crossed Ben's mind as he pulled up to the train tracks. He wondered if his neighbor, Mr. Brinkman, had dropped the bridge. Had he been in the area or taken part in the last stand he had found under the interstate?

Before Ben could think any further, Ian and Kelly came rushing around the corner. Kelly lost control of her bike, sliding the back wheel around before hitting the brakes hard. The maneuver ended up looking impressive. The look on her face told the story that she had, in fact, not meant to do the cool slide.

"Jesus," Ben said, watching the chests of the two heaving under the stress of intense riding. "You guys missed spin class?"

Kelly let out a chuckle between deep breaths. "I think we should leave and come check this out later."

"Or not," Ian followed. "Check out the bridge," Ian pointed out.

The water was coming perilously close.

"We can talk in the truck," Ben said as the three pedaled across the open space.

CHAPTER 10

The parking lot ramp looked to the crew like the finish line on a long, jar ring race. Stopping at the bottom entrance where Ben had pushed through the gate, they dismounted their bikes. Rainwater cascaded down the concrete building.

Ian and Kelly were still breathing hard as the three walked up the ramp. Much to Ben's delight, the truck was still there, and from what he could tell, untouched.

As soon as they walked under the cover of the parking garage, as if practiced, all three pulled back their hoods, letting out a deep breath.

"What happened?" Ben asked, opening the truck and putting his rifle in the driver's seat before walking around and opening the back.

"Just like I said. I'm not sure what happened to the person he walked into that garage, but by the looks of the surrounding area, it wasn't going to be good," Ian said, handing his bike to Ben.

"Could you see the person?" Ben asked, loading the bikes.

"No, they had a hood over their face. It looked like they had full shackles on. There was also a ton of headless zombies everywhere. We saw a few moving around but kept away from them. They looked like crazies. You know, not fully turned," Kelly replied as a door creaked open from inside the dark garage.

Ben pulled out his pistol as Kelly grabbed her rifle out of the passenger seat.

Ben again thought about how every dead zombie meant one less Sarah might run into. Another echo filled the void. This time from the other side of the bay.

"Ten minutes till travel alarm," Eve chirped happily, making Ben about jump out of his skin.

"Guys," Ben told them, walking over to the driver's side. "Get in."

Ian and Kelly did not hesitate in following his lead. The truck sprang to life. Ben flipped on the front lights, pulling slightly inward into the dark void to make a turn.

Ben would count this as one of the biggest mistakes he would make, at least as far as that day.

A wall of writhing gray flesh and snapping mouths greeted the headlights of the truck. Even worse, the wall of death was closing in, moving faster than Ben had yet to see a zombie move. Considering he had only been out for two days, he was left speechless.

"Drive!" Kelly yelled. "Now!"

Ben obliged, pushing down on the accelerator.

"Your heart rate is elevated. Would you like to listen to Pink Floyd?" Eve blared through the speakers.

The tires spun for a second before taking hold of the concrete, lurching the vehicle back in line down the ramp. Thumps reverberated off the back of the truck as the first of the zombies reached the fleeing vehicle.

The truck spun sideways as it slapped the remaining portion of the entrance gate. Water splashed up on the side of the vehicle as the truck spun around 180 degrees, landing in a large puddle of water leading out into the river.

"Shit, shit, shit," Ben repeated. The massive wall of gray bodies started cascading down the ramp, the front row slipping on the wet floor and falling over each other as Ben again pushed on the accelerator.

This time he made sure to pull out gracefully, genuinely believing that the man upstairs was giving him a break.

Pulling back out onto San Marco Boulevard, Ben continued to drive for a quarter-mile before pulling over and stopping, looking behind him to see no further evidence of the nightmare he had just witnessed.

Without saying a word, Ben pulled out his flask and took a longer than necessary pull. Looking at the two other passengers in his truck, he quickly realized their nerves had also been tested.

"Here," Ben said, reaching his flask out to Kelly. "Ladies first."

Kelly took the flask in her hand, taking a pull just as long and dedicated as Ben's had been. Ian sat there looking like a lost puppy, his eyes wide and the vein in his neck pumping from the overexertion of his heart.

She handed over the flask as Ian took it, finishing off what was left in the pint-size container.

"Any idea where the hell those things came from?" Ben asked as he gently pulled back out onto the main road. Pink Floyd quietly played in the background. Eve had taken his silence as a yes.

"I'm guessing they were there all along. All the rain probably had them distracted," Ian replied, adjusting the air conditioner vents in front of him to keep the cool air from blowing on his now wet clothes.

"I haven't seen a group of zombies like that together in a long time. It was like a smaller group peeled off and went into the parking garage. I wouldn't be surprised if someone had herded them in there at some point," Kelly said, taking a deep breath.

"What about the guy you two saw. Any idea about him?" Ben asked as he started picking up speed, now being moderately familiar with the road.

"We didn't want to stick around to find out. When the weather lets up, I wouldn't mind checking the place out to see what's going on. The creep had a radio hanging off his waist," Ian said, reaching his hand back and grabbing Kelly's.

The two genuinely loved each other, and it shone through in everything they did. The conversations they had and the actions they took toward each other reminded Ben of him and his wife, Sarah.

"Well, are we heading back to last night's safe house, or are we going to see what's behind door number two?" Ben asked.

Ian and Kelly were quiet for a few moments. "Tell you what;

take a right here, drive down to San Jose Boulevard, then take a right into Alhambra Drive," Ian said, obviously agreeing on something with Kelly.

The truck was going south on Hendricks Avenue as Ben took a slow right on one of the offshoot neighborhoods heading toward the river. He had forgotten how nice the neighborhoods were on the riverside of the street.

Mansions great and small lined the river, and while the houses in the subsequent neighborhoods were nice, they were nothing compared to what sat on the water.

Ben could relate as he slowly weaved around tree limbs, abandoned cars, and oddly, several trash cans in the middle of the roads, lying there just as if the owners had put the trash out to get picked up before they had evacuated.

"Is it safe back here?" Ben inquired as he looked over to Ian, seeing him nodding. It was clear they knew these roads well.

Ben took the final turn as he saw the houses at their destination. Visions of his house flooded his memories. He wanted to go home.

"Which one?"

"See the one with all the trees covering the front of the house making a sort of private drive with the gate? That one," Kelly pointed out.

Ben recognized the place. Families oftentimes went there to have pictures taken, and if memory served, he had been there for a wedding at one point.

"A+ for taste," Ben approved, pulling up to the gate and letting Ian out to open it. Ben noticed that the gate opened electronically. He looked back at Kelly. "This place has power?"

"Sort of," Kelly replied as Ian started walking down the drive, motioning Ben to follow. "There is a solar panel out back that powers the outdoor kitchen and the gate. It's pretty sparse, but it's our go-to. Any power these days is enough to probably start a war over."

Ben let that statement marinate. He was quickly realizing how special of a place he lived in.

The round driveway out front had a small feature that Ian rounded, motioning Ben to pull in front of the entrance. Ian had gotten out with his rifle and did a quick sweep of the front of the house before pulling what looked like a key out of his pocket, opening the door.

The rain had started to slow down, coming down in a spatter that was more annoying than drenching. Kelly jumped out, followed by Ben.

He took a few minutes to secure the vehicle, making sure that the doors were locked after grabbing his additional backpack, satellite phone, radios, rifle, pistol, and what he had not shown them yet, a box of high-quality rations from the back of the truck.

Ben walked to the front entrance as Ian and Kelly took off their overcoats, setting down their gear to dry off.

"Dinner's on me tonight," Ben said while holding up the box, gaining envious looks from the pair. It was clear they knew what he had in his hands. It was steak night; dehydrated steak, but still.

What the team hadn't expected after the jarring last couple hours was the scene out back behind the house. There were two or three different tiers leading down to the river.

The house was obviously elevated, with a pool on the first level, a smaller one on the second, and the third leading to an area where you could set out and lounge, plus a dock.

The water was up to the second level, waves starting to lap in the area close to the pool. If the rain kept up and the river swelled any more, the second tier and pool would be swallowed by the angry river. Ben figured that areas like Black Creek were already well above flood stage levels, as it was one of the first places to go.

"Jesus," Ian said, looking over at Kelly. "I haven't seen this much water in forever."

Ian's voice was stressed and showing signs of fraying after the long day. After looking around for only another minute, Ben realized that while the place was nice, unless it held some deep secrets, the two were on thin ice looking for a shoreline.

In all fairness, Ian and Kelly had stayed out of certain areas that they were sure wouldn't have supplies and pleasantries. After all the crappy movies and books they had read and seen throughout the years, truth be told, it wasn't the people they had to worry about; it was the actual, honest-to-God zombies.

The place was immaculately clean, minus the obvious dust that had accumulated over time while they hadn't been staying there. Furniture sat barren as chandeliers hung without cobwebs, proving that the house was, in fact, secure.

After another few minutes of contemplation while looking at the river, Ben turned to the two. "Let me see what you guys have out back with the power generator. I know a few things about them. Maybe we can see if there is anything we can either get hooked up or, if you guys want, maybe take with us," Ben said as he handed the box to Kelly.

A smile crossed Kelly's face as the three of them walked back into the main house, walking down three small, simple steps and into the middle-tier living room. The back side of the house was covered in glass, and as they walked further into the mansion, the sweet smell of vanilla filled the air from an obvious overabundance of candles that sat on all the tabletops.

"You guys put these candles here?" Ben asked as Ian opened the back door, letting a gust of wind into the lonely house.

"Yep," Kelly replied as she skipped over to Ian. "There was a bunch of food in the refrigerator and they had a pet that they left out, so things were a little gross. We cleaned up."

The three walked out to the back, standing under the cover of the living room and outdoor kitchen, which was just as decadent and nice as the inside.

Looking around, the outside seemed to be a little bit more in order than the inside. You could tell that they spent most of their time out under the cover of the lanai and extended space outside.

Ian walked over and flipped a switch. A small, dull light in the ceiling fan started to come to life above an outdoor island and kitchen area with several barstools sitting around it. Kelly set the box down as Ben continued to take in the scene.

It was clear to Ben that he would have issues when he went back home due to the water. He quickly understood why they had picked this specific house out of all the hundreds of others. Besides the flooding river and ominous gray sky, the view was amazing.

Kelly started to prepare the meals for the team, putting hydrated packages of steaks in the water-activated heaters.

"So, tell me about your other place," Ben said, sitting down at one of the stools on the island.

The countertop was high-end, black with gold speckles granite. In another time and age, he would have actually been envious of the outdoor living space and kitchen, considering that he himself lived in a small mansion. Ian figured that as long as he didn't tell him the location, it would be fun.

"It's like this place, but on the ocean. We have several more solar panels, but there's just enough energy for the fans and a few appliances. The problem with that house is that it was more or less a showpiece. It wasn't built for something like this. The owners — my parents, thought their money could buy them out of anything, so they didn't prepare for...the end of the world."

"I get it, but there have to be more houses around that area that have something that you could live off of. Coming all the way out here seems awfully dangerous," Ben said, pulling his flask out of his vest and setting it down on the island once he realized it was empty.

Ian quickly realized that Ben wasn't the only one who needed a drink. He ran off into the house only to appear moments later with a bottle of Deep Eddy vodka.

Drinks were mixed and consumed as they continued talking about Ian and Kelly's living situation. Much like Ian's parents, the majority of people around them hadn't thought of such things as preparing for zombies.

Kelly went on to talk about the different areas on the First Coast. They had not gone north of J. Turner Butler Boulevard, the main artery in Jacksonville heading from west to east into the beach.

It struck Ben as odd; however, he understood sticking to what you knew all too well.

The three intrepid survivors ate like kings that night, sitting under the covered lanai watching the rain come in, talking about the day's events. Ian and Kelly admitted that they had not seen a group as violent in their movements as they had in the parking garage in months.

This was also exacerbated by the fact that the large herd of zombies that had come through last night had been moving at an oddly quick pace, faster than they would usually expect.

"It's like something's getting them all wound up," Kelly commented as she leaned back in her stool, smacking her now full belly.

"That's what I was thinking," Ian agreed, sucking air through his teeth and clearing out strands of beef from between. The food had been good, and Ben attributed it to the high dollar they'd paid for it, making him grin slightly as they complimented the meal nonverbally. "Maybe something happened somewhere that we don't know about, and they're all fairly fresh, maybe even crazies with a few zombies sprinkled in. That guy we saw at the arena might very well be part of all this, or at least know what's going on."

Ben sat there speculating for a moment, taking another drink of his vodka mixed with cheap fruit punch that was on the verge of spoiling. "I've got a couple more stops I need to make at some point over the next week. If you guys help me get that done, we will all go back out and check out the arena."

Ian and Kelly nodded, not only approving of the plan but accepting it.

Eve interrupted the conversation by reminding Ben that it was getting close to sundown. Ian reassured Ben that the house was secure as he showed him upstairs to the living quarters.

The bedrooms were just as nice as the rest of the house, though the lack of air circulation led to a certain musty smell that could only be compared to a dirty hotel room.

Unlike the vanilla-scented allure of the downstairs open living area, the upstairs had been spared that luxury. But the beds were top quality, much like one would find in an upscale hotel room. Ben smiled, thinking about home. By the looks of things, Ben would have to wear pants from now on when he went out in the mornings.

CHAPTER 11

The morning proved to bring a significant improvement in the weather. Ben stretched as Eve reminded him it was time to get out of bed and grab a cup of coffee.

This morning there would be no automated energy dispenser waiting for them. That didn't stop him, however, as he had brought his own coffee-making kit.

Walking downstairs, it was obvious that Ian and Kelly had stayed up late that night. Ben started to brew the coffee using a small propane burner. The smell overtook the artificial vanilla scent lingering in the air. To be fair, the candles were high quality and more than likely legitimately real vanilla.

It didn't take long for the smell of freshly brewed coffee to stir the other inhabitants of the mansion.

"Wakie, wakie, no eggs or baki, but I got some really kick-ass coffee," Ben said, walking around the kitchen island, his Glock hanging off a shoulder holster he had grabbed out of his bag.

The morning prior, Ben hadn't felt comfortable going through his routine. This morning he would do as best he could. Eve was hooked up to a small Bluetooth speaker that Ben carried the size of an octagonal baseball. "Minerva" by the Deftones played coolly in the background. Even though the volume was low, the song reverberated smoothly off the open walls.

"You are a miracle," Ian said, walking up while stretching, also having a pistol in a shoulder holster.

"Look outside. Stands to reason the rain is slowing down. I've been looking for about thirty minutes, and I haven't seen a band go by. Hopefully, the trickle of rain we're seeing now is it," Ben informed them, slightly exasperated as the two drank their coffee while staring at the now underwater pool. The water was front and center on his mind.

"We heading south today?" Ian asked, not only wanting to know but also confirming to himself that they were, in fact, leaving with Ben.

The night prior, Ian and Kelly had asked Ben a few questions about where he lived. He had kept it simple, explaining it was a good place and, for some reason, felt like keeping the surprise. Today he would show them. Today they would see.

"Yep, as soon as we get up and get everything loaded, we're heading out. I forgot to turn on the sat phone last night. I'm planning on spending some time with it later today. Also, I have a little idea," Ben said, smirking as he took another sip of the rich coffee.

Ben went on to explain his plan as Kelly came downstairs. It was simple. The pair would talk through the radios, acting as if they didn't know each other and were talking from a distance, to see if they could get a reaction out of the people in the arena.

They would try a few channels above and a few channels below. Not only would this give them something to do on their trip out, it might also clarify a point. The point being to see if the people really wanted to talk or just draw others in.

Kelly again turned on the radio, listening to the repeating signal. Ben also turned on his on a separate channel, with the clicks coming through. "Hey, do you guys know Morse code?" Ben asked.

"I have a book on it. One of those survival books. Haven't really looked at it much, but we can figure it out," Ian said as he started collecting his things.

Ben set the radio on the table, letting the team hear the sequential clicks of the radio too.

"Is it just me or is there one too many messages on repeat out there?" Ben commented as he filled up his flask with vodka, taking a sip for good measure and calming his nerves. Kelly finished off her real coffee with a grin.

"Let me guess, you guys had been drinking the instant stuff," Ben said as Ian and Kelly nodded in affirmation. "You know, I bet we can still find some better dry sealed packet stuff in a grocery somewhere once everything calms down. Maybe we'll take a run out and see what we can find."

The music coming from the bluetooth speaker ground to a halt as Ben clicked the top button, putting Eve back on his wrist. "Time to get this party going," Ben said. The command shut Eve down, basically putting her on vibrate mode.

After gathering their things, the three stepped outside. Rain still spattered off their shoulders as gray clouds hid the morning sun from the crew. They piled into the truck as Ben started the ignition, bringing life to the vehicle that had separated them from certain death the day prior.

"You think we're gonna run into anything today?" Kelly asked.

"With all this rain, I'm not sure what we'll see. I was almost thinking it might be better just to stay put for a few more days, but Ben here is hell-bent on getting home. If he's going to take us, I'm willing to take the risk," Ian said assuredly.

Ian looked back at the house as they pulled out after closing the gate. Ben knew that look. Ian was giving their on-again, off-again sanctuary a final appreciative glance.

The rain was still present. However, it had slowed down to an annoying trickle. Blue sky and rays of midmorning sun danced in the distance. Ben wasn't oblivious to the fact that the water could still be rising.

A little over a year ago, he could've gotten to the front gates of his humble abode in well under an hour. Today, depending on what they encountered, it would take several hours.

By Ben's measure, he hadn't taken the truck over 15 mph the whole trip, minus the initial burst of speed from the parking garage. In all fairness, that area had been unobstructed.

"So, we stopping anywhere on the way back?" Kelly asked, leaning forward between the two men in the front seat.

"No, not if we can avoid it. I was planning on it but would rather check on the house. You guys ready to do this radio thing?" Ben said, changing the subject.

It was clear his two passengers were more comfortable with making stops. This was, of course, due to their need to scavenge for supplies, and in many ways, even though he didn't need the extra things, he saw the inviting thrill of the hunt — minus the zombies.

While weaving in and out of cars, heading back toward San Jose Boulevard, they again timed the gap between messages from the arena. There was a simple two-minute pause between every repeating cadence of the welcoming voice.

"Hello, is anyone there?" Kelly said, quickly clicking the radio off and giggling, showing her youth.

"Hello, who is this? This is Jimmy. Can you hear me?" Ian played along, responding to Kelly's message as if he didn't know who she was. Ian also followed up with a light chuckle and grin after letting go of the radio.

The recorded message came across the radio again as Kelly kept talking a few more times to make it seem as if she was trying to open up a conversation.

On cue, Ian responded back after the message ended. "Are you still there? Hello?" Ian asked in a more desperate tone. "Whoever is there, I think this is a recorded message."

"I can hear you loud and clear. This is Tina." Kelly and Ian were obviously having fun making up their separate identities.

"Thank God. My name is Jimmy," Ian repeated as the click of a third radio drew them into silence.

Shallow breathing could be heard on the radio before it was quickly clicked off, as if someone was deciding whether to talk or not. Their question had been answered. Someone was, in fact, monitoring that radio channel, and they would use it to figure out who that person was at the arena.

The radio continued to click off and on as if somebody was deciding whether to talk or not for the next five minutes as the truck eased back out on San Jose Boulevard.

A large, foot-deep puddle covered the intersection as   Ian held his hand out, pointing down at the edge of the road to signal that there was another strip. If Ben wasn't careful, they would indeed be spending the night out again together. The team gave the radio play a break as silence filled the air.

"So, what did you do before all this, Ben?" Kelly asked from the back seat. This was a question that he had not planned on answering but knew he would be asked. It was clear to Kelly that his backstory of being a soldier, while he absolutely looked the part and handled himself just as well, it was not the backdrop in which Ben had spent his young adult life.

Ben took a deep breath. "It's a little complicated," Ben evaded, truly wondering if he could trust the two to tell them the story. He hadn't even let his neighbors or newer friends in on his past.

"Ever since we ran into you, something's been nagging me. You look awfully familiar," Ian spoke, grinning that youthful smile that would have once upon a time been right at home on a long, sunny day hanging at the beach.

"I get that a lot. Well, used to. I was in the entertainment business; I'll leave it at that. Before that mess, I grew up in the country. My dad was a marine. That's why I know how to shoot and handle myself for the most part. I had to grow up on my own as he was always gone," Ben explained, giving them just enough but not everything.

"Oooooh, we got us a famous mystery man," Kelly joked, the two picking up that I wasn't in the mood to talk about it.

"Ha-ha, and all that," Ben replied, squinting and leaning forward in his seat to look between wipes of the windshield blades. "Take a look at that. Isn't that the turnoff to your other house where I screwed up my tire?" Ben was still planning on coming back later for the gear he had left behind. Just not today.

The truck came to a halt as all three of them leaned forward in their seats as if they had synchronized the movement.

"That's not good," Ian broke the silence, his mood shifting from relaxed and jovial to concerned and slightly hardened.

A car sat on the curb, having hit the same spike strips at a high rate of speed. All four doors were open as red and brown streaks adorned most of what once must've been white paint.

"People?" Ben asked, reaching down to his chest to ensure his pistol was there.

"Zombies, and by the looks of it, pissed-off ones," Kelly replied. The silence was replaced with the rattle of guns and clicks.

The trio was getting ready just in case. "Look over there," she pointed at a few bodies of obvious zombies. They weren't moving. "D.D." is what Ian and Kelly called them, meaning "Double Dead."

"I would have thought most of them had left with the main group the night before. Like I was saying, something's been weird about how they've been moving around lately," Ian said, pulling the rifle from the back after working the action on his pistol.

"I don't think we should stick around to find out. By the looks of that vehicle, I don't think whoever was in it is going to be anywhere around here or alive," Ben said, making a point as he looked over at his passengers, seeing their acceptance and approval.

Ben again put the vehicle into motion, driving past the gruesome scene. Two mangled, recently deceased bodies lay off the road behind the vehicle, out of sight from their previous location. Reality struck home as his determination to go back solidified even further.

He was amazed that Sarah had survived as long as she had out on her own. Was she on her own? Ben thought to himself. Hopefully, she had found a group of people much like Ian and Kelly to travel with.

Thoughts of her traveling with a muscle-bound security officer from CDC also crossed Ben's mind before he quickly pushed that thought out of his head.

After another twenty minutes, the mood and the truck started to ease. There were no further signs of zombies besides the trampled bushes and what was once grass.

The road in most places had a couple of inches of standing water. After a year or so of the storm drains not being cleaned and already being susceptible to flooding in the area, Ben was surprised they were able to go anywhere.

What seemed like a beacon of victory loomed on the horizon. The I-295 overpass. Ian and Kelly simply called it the south. It got Ben's heart racing.

"It's time for your afternoon nap. You may want to listen to some calming music; your heart rate is elevated," Eve said, breaking the last thirty minutes of awkward silence as even Ben joined in snickering at the distraction.

Ben once again brought the truck to a stop as the gas station from his previous encounter loomed not too far in front of the vehicle to the right.

"What's up?" Ian asked as he reached down, pulling a beef stick out of his pocket.

"You see the gas station up there? That was the one I was telling you about, where I got the beer and ran into that zombie that got a little too close. That red truck wasn't there when I left. I think this rain's gotten more than the zombies out and about," Ben said.

While he truly didn't know the day-to-day goings-on outside the walls of his castle, he had quickly realized that things in the regular world moved much slower. After all, Ian and Kelly had noticed things had been moved after being away for several weeks.

They also knew the patterns of the zombies and could literally tell Ben where to turn and not turn while they were talking without looking at the road.

"We never really come down here. Too close to the south. I couldn't tell you what looks out of place down here," Ian said, confirming Ben's thoughts.

Kelly pulled out a pair of binoculars and leaned between the two men, staring into the distance at the gas station. The three of them, in a few short days had become a dysfunctional family and team of sorts.

Ben backed the truck up several feet behind some overgrown trees. For some reason, he had stopped before pulling up on the gas station.

"I don't see any signs of zombies; I can't see any bodies lying around either. The vehicle could be out of gas, and they were just looking for some fuel. Or they could still be around there," Kelly said, handing the binoculars to Ben.

"What do you think?" Ian asked him. In all fairness, Ben hadn't told them that this was his first trip out.

For all they knew, he had all the answers. One thing was for sure. They absolutely believed the story about him being on his own, not questioning if this was some kind of a setup.

"Yeah, I think whoever it is, is in that store. Look, two new friends are enough for me this week. I'm not out trying to pick up every stray dog and cat off the street. If everyone around here is as scared to go south of I-295 as you say they are, I'm gonna blow down this road as fast as we can. It's probably the clearest stretch we're going to see until we get to where we're going. If they try to come after us, that probably means bad news. If they don't, we just pay a little bit more attention next time we're out," Ben said as Ian pulled out an old smartphone, zooming in and snapping a picture of the truck.

Ian and Kelly looked at each other, both without saying anything, agreeing to Ben's plan. Truth be told, as they had discussed before, the movies and the books often got it wrong.

They figured it was either due to the fact that only a year had gone by or that people were still actually organizing to take on the zombie threat, but most people that Ian and Kelly had ran into were in fact nice people. Ben's first encounter with new folks had also been fruitful and positive.

"Right, everybody buckle up just in case the road's still wet," Ben ordered, looking down at the power meter on the truck. Pushing the vehicle would drain the batteries that much faster.

Technology had come a long way; he could easily get three or four hundred miles on the charge and small tank of fuel that the vehicle held if needed. After being outside of his secluded paradise, Ben was quickly realizing that recharging the truck would not be a simple task. Ben briefly paused, taking another look at the gas station. A larger man looking to be in his mid-forties walked out the door carrying several cases of beer.

Holding up a finger, the other two leaned forward in their seats.

"What is it?" Ian asked, chewing annoyingly on his snack, the smell of spices filling the cab.

Ben reached down, pulling his flask out and unscrewing the top with his thumb, taking two pulls. "Looks to me like the guy's on a beer run. I don't think he saw us. Change of plans."

The truck slowly pulled further back off the road and into the parking lot, where there were two vehicles flipped on their sides next to a group of overgrown palms. Ben slowly crept the truck between the two and cut it off.

"We're going to wait here until he passes. He's either gonna go south, or right up this road. I don't think he's going to take any other turns. With luck, he won't even know or around now," Ben said, taking a deep breath, his chest heaving.

"What do they look like?" Kelly asked as she smacked Ian on the shoulder, motioning for a snack.

"I mean, normal, I guess. He looked strong, big. He's been eating well. I couldn't make it out, but I think he had a gun and a radio; I can't be sure." Ben had pulled back before handing the binoculars over to Ian or Kelly to see. If he had, things might've changed.

As if ordered by the gods, the red pickup truck went north on San Jose Boulevard. Whoever was operating that red truck knew the area just as well as Ian and Kelly, driving faster than Ben felt comfortable to.

One thing was obvious to Ben, however, and he made it perfectly clear to the others. No one had been in that service station before he had two days prior.

"How long before we leave?" Ian asked as Ben looked down at Eve.

Before Ben could get the words out of his mouth, a loud thump smacked the back of the truck. None of them had been paying attention to the rearview mirrors. The windows had become fogged from their conversation and the trickling rain outside.

Another thump came around the truck as the three started to look around, wildly wiping the windows off. Movement to the right, coming out of the bushes, signaled that they weren't alone. Another thump, and the vehicle shook.

Without hesitation, Ben brought the truck back to life, putting it in drive and moving forward faster than he could register what was happening. Lumbering bodies emerged from the tree line where they had sat earlier, watching the red truck.

"Shit, shit, shit!" Ben hissed out. There were dozens of bodies everywhere. Zombies.

As quickly as a raindrop could hit the windshield, dozens of zombies surrounded the truck as if out of nowhere. It shocked them how fast the group had converged on the vehicle without them knowing. The combination of light rain, fogged-up windows, and overall crappy conditions were partly to blame.

A bloody arm slammed into the driver's side window, startling Ben and making Kelly flinch. It was as if the clouds had opened up, and it was raining zombies. Ben was more confused than panicked with the quickness with which they had been engulfed by the swarm.

These were crazies; fresh and not fully turned. He had learned much from his new companions, the main thing being that there were two types of the damn things, and seeing blood was a telltale sign of a crazy not fully gone but gone enough.

Kelly had even said that while they were crazies, they still kept some of their prior habits, things like going to a place they knew, even home. Kelly had also stated that she had witnessed one try to get in a car and drive, only to rip the steering wheel off, the force of the blunt instrument lodging into its own skull killing the thing instantly.

One of the creatures scratched the truck as it was knocked back, the truck running over its legs with a teeth-jarring crack. Ben knew that while he wanted nothing more than to ram through them, it didn't take much to get even the toughest vehicle stuck if confronted with enough obstacles.

He had also read in a comic book about zombies that running

over one with something as simple as a pair of blue jeans on could get it caught in the axle and tires, causing a general shitstorm of additional problems.

"Look out!" Kelly shrieked as Ben slammed into a man dressed to go to the gym.

The truck rocked as the tires crushed the brittle body. The sound of popping and crunching, much like eating celery, reverberated in the truck to the point that the passengers could feel it.

Ben cut the wheel to the left only to realize that several more zombies had come out from behind the overturned vehicles he had reversed and slipped behind.

Ian cracked the window as he pulled his rifle out, letting out several bursts and deafening the crew inside the cab. Shell casings ricocheted off the seat and window, bouncing around the cab.

Clack, clack, clack! Again, Ian's rifle barked. Several zombies to the right dropped on the road as if somebody had just pushed the off button, simply making them stop. He was good. Not only was Ian a crack shot, but he had only taken a few seconds to react.

"Go right!" Ian exclaimed as he again unleashed the M4 he was holding. By this time, Ben's ears were ringing, however he had enough adrenaline going through his system to allow him to hear.

Turning right, Ben pushed the accelerator hard again, crunching over several bodies and creating the same sound and sensation as earlier. The perseverance and aggressiveness of the truck impressed Ben.

In a rush of violence and speed, the truck spat out into San Jose Boulevard. Ian quickly pulled in his rifle, rolling up the window pointing his fingers in a forward motion. Ben didn't look behind to see the carnage left, only focused on the path forward.

The truck smoothly drove under the overpass of I-295 as Ben reached down and handed the flask over to Ian and Kelly. There was no point in talking; their ears rang loudly from the weapon being discharged within the vehicle. Ian hadn't had the time to lean out of the window, and for that, the team was forever grateful, even though their ears were paying the price.

Ben stopped the truck in the middle of the road just before getting to the Julington Creek bridge. Opening the door, Ben threw up.

While he had acted calm, the incident had, in fact, rattled his nerves even more so than the previous days. If it wasn't for Ian, they would more than likely still be stuck back there.

"What's up?" Ian asked, walking around with his rifle in front of him. "My nerves. Man, that was close," Ben replied, taking a deep breath, feeling better.

"Yeah, but did you die?" Ian joked, not getting a reaction.

"Thanks. Look, I'm glad we found each other," Ben admitted, meaning every word of what he had just stated. "I'm just afraid we're going to run into a little bit more trouble trying to get the rest of the radios out. I'm starting to think about what might be the best option."

Ben had driven the last half mile in ringing silence, thinking about the docked boats and the small flats boat he had back home.

Ian just nodded in agreement. He hadn't been this far south since the shit hit the fan. From everything he had heard people say, this should be a complete war zone. But everyone was wrong.

The storefronts, for the most part, looked intact. Looting had been minimal, as had been the large-scale standoffs that had happened in other parts closer to the city. Ian was starting to wonder if some of this was to keep people away from the spoils, or if there was, in fact, no one down here left.

Ben, finally getting his footing, stood up straight. He dwarfed Ian. Between the muscle and height, it was surprising to Ian that he was not more aggressive. It was noticeably clear Ben could handle himself.

"You thinking what I'm thinking?" Ian asked Ben as the two looked behind them.

"Yeah, we need to get a boat," Ben said as Ian nodded.

Ben had seen enough of the roads. He knew what Sarah was dealing with, and he would only be able to do so much. His adage of each zombie killed being one less she had to deal with was starting to become less important. He figured that after a year being out on her own, she knew how to handle herself and avoid getting into tough situations.

Ben felt guilty. While Sarah was out surviving, he had been cozily tucked away having cocktails while listening to Pink Floyd, watching the sunset every afternoon.

The two men got back in the cab of the truck. Kelly was playing with the radio again, talking and acting like her character Tina. No one on the other side was clicking or responding back, however, as the message started to repeat over again.

"Ben, have you checked out any of the stores around here?" Kelly asked as she clicked the radio off.

"To be crystal clear with you, I've never had a need to. That might change in the near future, but for now, the only thing I'm really interested in is the battery shop we just passed," Ben said.

"Do you want to go check it out before we get back?" Ian asked. Everybody's hearing was coming back to some form of normalcy.

"I just want to get back. When we come out to hit the Buckman, I'm planning on it," Ben said.

Starting the truck again, Ben looked down to see the battery meter slowly lowering. While he hadn't traveled hundreds of miles, the vehicle nonetheless had been on and running, draining precious energy from the truck. He shoved that thought off, knowing he would soon be home and able to plug the vehicle back up to the panels and generator.

The team reached the Julington Creek bridge as Ben noticed something. Besides the still-rising water, the BMW he had run into before that looked much like his neighbor's now had the doors open.

It was odd to Ben that he was now starting to see things the same way as Ian and Kelly. Small details seemed to stand out in an otherwise permanently frozen world. He stopped the truck again.

"Need some more fresh air?" Ian asked.

"No, you see that BMW? When I came through here last time, the doors were closed, shut tight. They're open now. Someone's been here. As you can see, not many folks have been down here. When I drove north, I could tell I was the first to drive that road in a long, long time."

"We've passed hundreds of cars. Why this one?" Ian interjected.

"I'm fairly sure you guys noticed a leaf out of place back there, minus all the rain. This thing is in the middle of the bridge, and I swear to god I think I know the old owner," Ben said, a mild hate for the man growing in his chest. What he had found in his house was beyond acceptable. He was glad he was likely dead. "Anyway, someone's been by. The car's just on the bridge, so there's no doubt it stuck out more than the others."

Ben and Ian looked back at the truck. The once pristine vehicle was now covered in gore and whatever else had clung to it over the past couple of days. Neither wanted to admit how close they had come to not making it out of their hiding spot. That was twice in a short period of time.

The damn things had been hiding in the tree line. Ian explained how they didn't like the sunlight, and of all the lessons he had learned recently, Ben would not forget this one.

The smell of the brackish water of the St. Johns River permeated from below the bridge. The rain had stopped, and as Florida was noticeably famous for, the humidity was starting to take hold.

Ben got back in the truck, reflecting on the fairly clear drive he remembered they had ahead.

CHAPTER 12

"How much farther?" Ian asked his impatience with Ben's vagueness coming through in his voice.

"Another five miles or so, maybe a little more. It's a clear drive the rest of the way down. We'll get off the main drag and onto the county road soon enough. There's debris in the road, but on a whole, not much of anything else. Only thing I'm worried about is the water. It's still not crested, and I'm sure some of the roads are going to flood soon if they haven't already," Ben said, calming as well as concerning Ian.

"Flood? Isn't that bad?" Ian said, worry showing through his voice. "We're getting close enough, so that's not going to be an issue. There's nothing much down here but a few neighborhoods sprinkled here and there. Trees and damn swamp on one side and water on the other," Ben said, reassuring the two.

While not completely sure after what he'd seen in the past couple of days, there was a low probability of anything being in the tree lines besides a few stragglers. They would stay on the road.

The three rode in silence as the sun lightly shone between the trees now covering the two-lane road. They had been driving for what felt like forever before a grin started to spread across Ben's face.

Ben pulled over to the side of the road in an indistinct area. Upon closer examination, Ian and Kelly could see the brush that had been pulled over the nondescript turnoff. Just as Ben had thought, if you were driving by and didn't know it was there, you wouldn't notice it.

"Home sweet home!" Ben exclaimed as the pair looked at each other. "So, we're going camping?" Ian asked, a slight twitch of nervousness coming through in his voice.

"Oh, this is big money down through here," Kelly interjected. She was moderately familiar with the area, and the statement made that extremely clear.

Ian got out, helping Ben move the brush out of the entrance. After a few moments of maneuvering, Kelly pulled the truck through the opening as Ben and Ian put the brush back in place for the additional optics. It didn't take long for the two visitors to understand what Ben was hiding.

The gates to the neighborhood stood resolute, ivy growing over the sides and edges as far as they could see to either side. Ben got out, walking over to a small security pad and punching in a couple of buttons. There was an audible click, proving to Ian and Kelly that Ben did, in fact, have power.

The lock was something that Ben had rigged to have power on; opening the gate was another story as he had to do that manually. As Ben pulled the gate open, Kelly pulled the truck through, stopping and rolling the window down.

"Holy shit, no wonder you are trying to keep this place a secret. It's damn near hidden," Kelly said, her excitement starting to bubble over.

"When you turn on that main road, it's the second house on your left. You can't miss it; there's a white parapet on top of the house with a small cross," Ben said, trying not to give everything away.

"Yeah, I think I can see it from here," Ian said, rolling his eyes in a jokingly manner.

Ben looked around his private paradise. He had been worried that he would see water as he opened the gate, but none was to be found in front of the houses. Behind them, he knew it would be a different story and also knew that the water would probably continue to rise.

Maybe they would get lucky and, with all the craziness going on, the river was blocked further upstream. Several scenarios crossed his mind as he stood there taking it all in, glad to be back. Something was still bothering Ben, however. Something in the back of his mind.

It was the feeling you got when you lost your car keys only to find them an hour later in a place you knew for a fact you hadn't left them. Taking a deep breath, he shrugged it off as just the drastic change his life had taken over the past week.

Part of him wanted to go back out immediately and set up the other radios as soon as he could. The other half didn't want to go out and see the chaos that he had just left again.

The three of them all converged on the front door of Ben's house. He hadn't thought about it, but his humble abode in fact was nicer than the one they had stayed at last night. Maybe not as showy, but it was modern, sleek, and absolutely expensive.

Ben lifted the cover on the security keypad in which he had a key to open the stainless-steel security box, punching in several digits as the sound of locking mechanisms retracting and magnets loosening filled the humid air.

The sights, sounds, and smells of Ben's house immediately caught the two off guard. Eve linked up to Ben's house-wide wireless system immediately, her voice lightly coming over the speakers built into the ceiling while welcoming Ben home.

"Eve, coffee, please," Ben stated.

"Absolutely," Eve replied. Ben walked into the front entrance hall and noticed that Ian and Kelly were still standing outside, taking in the scene. He had power, he had lights, and most importantly, he had good coffee.

The three converged on the kitchen as people often did, the smell of freshly brewed coffee filling the air. He had left one of the large automatic coffee machines on the counter ready for just this occasion when he came through the door. Ben walked over to the refrigerator and opened the door.

While he hadn't left the rest of the systems on, the main refrigerator had remained powered up while he was gone. Ben had figured that since he wasn't running any other main systems, he could let some water cool and possibly even make some ice.

Two pitchers of ice-cold water sat in front of him. Ben pulled them out, putting them on the counter before grabbing three glasses and hitting the ice dispenser on the other side.

The tinkling sound of ice was accompanied by the grinding of the actual ice maker popping the cubes neatly in the glasses. The refrigerator itself had cost Ben and Sarah at least $10,000, but it made the good stuff.

Ian and Kelly grabbed the glasses, holding them before drinking the water as if they were about to die. The two started laughing, crunching on ice and looking at each other almost simultaneously. Small pleasures like ice water were a rarity, and probably one of the most basic things they had taken for granted prior to everything happening.

Ben joined in as the coffee maker dinged. The smell of roasted beans filled the air as Ian's and Kelly's senses were tantalized. Pulling down three mugs, Ben set them on the table next to the ice-cold water, pouring the coffee and reaching into the cupboard to grab sugar packets.

"If you pull out creamer, I'm going to have a heart attack," Kelly joked as Ben reached back into the refrigerator to grab one of the three remaining items sitting inside.

While Ben had not yet used even a portion of his food stores, he had opened a condiment box that included powdered creamer. He had mixed it before he'd left and put it in the refrigerator to keep and set.

Ben grinned from ear to ear as the pair just sat there blowing out long, deep breaths of enjoyment. "What do you guys think?" Ben asked as everyone took their first sips of the delectable coffee.

"We've only been here a couple of minutes, and I've seen more than I've seen in the past seven months. That's when things really broke down," Ian explained, almost downing his cup of coffee on his second pull and going for a refill.

"You have power?" Kelly asked, interested and admiring at the same time. "Yup," was all Ben replied. He was enjoying seeing the two happy. It made him happy.

"What about the other houses?" she followed, which was a valid question.

"We can talk about all that after we get settled back in. Let's get the truck unloaded; I want to see how the water's looking outback. I even have a surprise for you. Hot showers," Ben said, reaching down his vest and pulling out his flask, taking a victory pull.

"I'll drink to that," Ian replied as Ben handed him the flask, Kelly following with the same comment. The three of them enjoyed a celebratory drink. What they were celebrating was a mystery, but they knew it was an occasion to celebrate.

After thirty minutes of unloading their gear, the three walked out back to see the water situation. As suspected, the current was about to cover all the docks.

Houses in a neighborhood such as Ben's had fill dirt brought in and were built several feet above sea level. This afforded certain luxuries, including pools and safety from flooding. Ben knew if the water kept rising, it could possibly get into the house, or even worse, the battery storage units close to the water.

Most of the storage batteries were in a small separate house, with the cables running underground and a few aboveground toward the solar panels.

Most of the food stores were in the house, but there was still a good amount stored in the battery house.

The three went back to the kitchen. Ben hadn't realized how bad they all smelled until they were in the house. The fans blew as Ben opened a few windows, enjoying the nice, breezy afternoon. The sun was covered by clouds, warding off the humidity they'd run into earlier.

"This place is amazing," Kelly complimented as she looked around, taking in every inch of the space. "You wouldn't even know it was here unless, well... you knew it was here. You have power, and from what I could tell, that gate goes from waterline to waterline, containing the inlet. This place is perfect; it's even defendable."

That last statement was one of the reasons Ben had brought

the two along, especially after being out the past couple of days. While it felt like an entire state away, Ben was in fact not that far from everything he had just experienced. Ben sat down and told them the story of how the house had come to be.

Ian and Kelly, at some point during the conversation, moved closer to each other, realizing why Ben was doing what he was doing. He was a good person, and so were they.

By the end of the conversation, Ian and Kelly were completely floored at not only Ben's preparedness but the fact that no one had found his hidden paradise. They also understood he wanted to keep it that way, and after seeing what he had in the short amount of time they'd been there, they agreed.

"Tell you what; the water heater's tankless. I can't run it for more than ten minutes at a time without it seriously draining the batteries. With all the rain recently, I'm quite sure the house is running off the stored power and is just now starting to charge back up. The pump will be fine as it's ran on a separate system. I'll make sure everything's in running order, and we should all be taking nice, warm showers within the next ten minutes.

"For now, you two can stay in the guest room on the first floor. Run the water for a couple of minutes before you jump in the shower; I haven't used that line in some time. I used to turn all the water spigots on, but I haven't done that one in at least a month. Oh, and help yourself to the toilets; I stocked up on toilet paper on my initial stop," Ben said bragging, feeling good about giving some of what he had and hoping some of his guilt would dissipate.

Ian and Kelly were still mildly in shock. The place was like a hotel, and they felt as if they were checking in. In private, the two made their minds up that they would do whatever they had to do to carry their weight.

After showers and a change of clothes, Ben explained the neighborhood more. There were generators in the other houses, but nothing like Ben's. They could stay in the house till he reunited with Sarah, then they would simply figure it out from there.

Ian and Kelly even stated that they would check the other houses out. Ben agreed, warning them to stay away from two of the houses: the one he had run into Mrs. Brinkman, at least for now, and the house that the younger neighbor, more specifically the one that drove the BMW, lived in. He didn't say more, and they didn't ask.

Ian convinced Ben that they would clean out the house if they chose to go to Mrs. Brinkman's, and the body needed to be removed anyway.

"One last thing," Ben started, remembering his floating visitor. "Before I left, a body washed up. He wasn't a zombie; someone had killed him. Shot in the heart with an arrow."

The pair looked at each other, pondering. "Have you heard a lot of boats on the river?" Ian asked, taking a sip from the second pot of coffee Eve had produced. It was the type of coffee maker where you put the beans on top of the machine, grinding away on command. A water line from the house's water system was hooked up to it, feeding Ben a constant source of go-juice.

"No, not that I can think of. Unless I was paying attention, there would be a good chance that I'd miss it," Ben said as he yawned.

"We haven't really heard about anything south of I-295. Like we said the other day, even the folks we've ran into on the beach or around the city have no clue," Kelly said, also picking up on Ben's yawn and joining in.

"How many people have you run into?" Ben inquired now that he figured all the cards were on the table.

"A dozen or so in the past six months. Everyone's pretty much in the same boat as we. I think that guy we saw downtown is the only person we haven't walked up and talked to. That's the one thing that's been worrying us: when will everybody else become desperate," Ian responded.

Ben wasn't stupid. He knew that the zombie shows and comic books, which had eventually ended up turning into how-to manuals, would more than likely become true at some point.

"People are going to get desperate at some point. I don't think I want to see that," Ben remarked, not only making an observation but a rule as well.

The rest of the evening found the three of them sitting out on the back lanai, drinking iced cocktails and watching the water, hoping it would crest soon.

CHAPTER 13

An alarm went off at roughly five in the morning. This wasn't the normal alarm that Ben was used to, and it startled him awake instantly. He was in the comfort and security of his own paradise. This alarm was something new.

Ian and Kelly joined Ben in the kitchen as they all looked around. There was nothing to justify the alarms going off. Ben quickly ran into his office and grabbed the laptop, playing it up to the house's smart system.

With the computer, Ben would immediately be able to see where the alarm was and also what it was for. It was all part of the prepper package, no Internet required.

The sun still hadn't come up, and before Ben could say anything, a flashing red warning sign labeled "battery purge" blinked on the screen. Ben started to panic.

Running to the back door, Ben opened it to be immediately greeted by water. It was only a few feet away from the door and was perilously close to flooding the back of the house.

"Shit," Ben cursed under his breath as the light flickered again.

"What's wrong?" Ian asked as he took in the river that had obviously swelled significantly overnight.

"The main batteries are in the boathouse in the backyard," Ben said, running back into the kitchen and grabbing a high-powered LED headlamp, placing it on, beaming its light onto the small house.

While they called it the boathouse, it wasn't next to the dock. It was twenty feet from the back of the house and roughly two feet below grade.

"The system's set to purge the batteries if they get submerged in water. There's also a shunt trip that's..." Ben started to explain as the lights finally gave way, going out.

"What do we do?" Kelly asked, worry evident in her voice.

"It will only purge if the batteries get wet. They're set up in sections. Hopefully, that was just one row of batteries," Ben said, wading out into the water.

The humid air and mosquitoes attacked Ben almost immediately. While the rain had stopped, the afternoon sun and rising water had generated the perfect Florida insect party. The loud sounds of frogs also peppered the night air. Luckily for Ben, the sun would soon be up; however, that would bring its own challenges.

Ben opened the boathouse door to see the bottom row of batteries submerged completely underwater, sparks coming from a short circuit in the far end of the boathouse.

"Worst case scenario, you lose three sectors," Ben whispered to himself, remembering the manual.

The first row was one sector. If he were to lose another, he would more than likely also lose the first floor of his house. Ben couldn't believe his luck, not only this morning but over the past week.

A sinking feeling slammed straight into Ben's chest as he stood there, looking at the room. The food stored in the boathouse was at least on a tall shelf in the back, not generating any immediate concern.

He squinted his eyes, looking at nothing, the headlamp's light dancing around, reflecting off the murky water. Ben suddenly took a deep, calming breath, clearing his mind and remembering what the manual said to do.

"Ian, Kelly," Ben yelled, calling the two over, who had also located lights in one of the drawers. Sunlight teased the sky, slightly taking the edge of the night off.

"Look, all we have to do is take the second sector out. If water gets to the top sector, it's not gonna matter. This whole place will be underwater," Ben said, pointing at the clamps on either side of the batteries lined up in a row.

"That's a hell of a lot of batteries," Ian observed as Ben unclipped the first one.

"Did you like taking a hot shower yesterday?" Ben asked as the others put their asses in motion immediately.

Forty-five minutes later, they had removed all the batteries from the second sector. The sun was now out; however, it wasn't fully reaching the house over the tree line yet. Ben poured three tall glasses of ice water as they sat in the kitchen looking at each other.

A green light flashed on the laptop, registering that the power grid was now stable and requesting any rerouting commands. Ben clicked the button to turn off the refrigerator and instead left on the plugs and fans in the house so he could do simple tasks such as make a pot of coffee.

"Do you think we're good?" Kelly asked, drinking the water and already pouring herself another, enjoying the icy, refreshing drink after the past hour of sweaty work.

"You know, I think we are. The water hasn't gone up anymore since this whole fiasco started. If it was still rising, it would be in the kitchen by now," Ben answered, nodding his head in affirmation.

"What about the batteries we pulled out of there? Should we wait until later today or tomorrow to put all those damn heavy things back?" Ian asked.

"Jesus, you guys are asking a lot of questions. Look, I think I'm going to wait till tomorrow to reinstall them. If memory serves, we can put half of the batteries in sector one and half in sector two. That will allow us to run all the things I have hooked up, just not at max power. Things like taking hot showers might be out of the question for a few days. The batteries are made to withstand water. That's why they dumped their cores or whatever you call it.

"I was planning on stopping by that battery store and picking more up. I know they used to carry them in stock; they had quite a few in the back. I mean, it's nothing more than high-grade battery acid at the end of the day, something like that. Good thing is, the pump's on a completely different system. The water would have to reach the top of the house for it to get that one," Ben explained, calming not only his nerves but those of the pair.

A loud ding coming from the bag sitting on the counter next to the stove startled the team.

Ben jumped out of his seat, rushing to the counter and pulling out the satellite phone. Looking down, he saw an actual honest-to-God text message. Not a short, quick note but an actual message. It was from Sarah.

He had turned the phone on last night and had forgotten to turn it off after his tenth cocktail and being distracted by his newfound friends.

He immediately shook his head, remembering the reason why Eve was so important. She kept him on schedule and in line, avoiding issues like completely draining the batteries on the phone before he could charge them, possibly deleting the encrypted programming of the phone.

The other two stood there staring.

Ben ranted to himself, mumbling under his breath while staring at the phone intently. Before he forgot, he grabbed the charging cable and plugged it immediately into the side of the laptop.

Ben,

I'm in a spot that has a full signal. I hope you get this; it's showing that you are getting and checking what I've sent. Look, the satellite phones only work well once a month during the full moon; they can work intermittently at least once a week, but if you hit it on the night of the full moon, the phone should work just fine after midnight and before 5:00 a.m.

Ben thought momentarily, remembering that last night had been a full moon.

I'm in Tallahassee with a group of people. They know I'm a doctor and don't want me to leave. It's getting complicated here. People are beginning to get desperate. I'm telling you this just in case we get cut off. We're at the Capitol building downtown. They still have power. Stick to the plan. I'll know if you read this message in a few days. Try using the phone around 1:00 a.m. a week from today. You should be able to at least get a word or a few letters through. I know it doesn't make a lot of sense, but neither are the satellites now, considering nobody's manning them. Look, if the plan is not complete in thirty days, there is an issue.

Love, Sarah

After reading the message out loud, his two new companions sat back, letting out a breath for Ben, as he was still holding his in.

"What the hell does that mean?" Ben fumed. His temper had flared at the thought of someone keeping his dear Sarah from him.

"Sounds like she's being cryptic for a reason," Kelly replied, planting that seed in Ben's mind. He had thought that same thing with the previous message.

Was someone monitoring her messages? No, they would have just taken the phone. Sarah was smart. Even if they had tried, she would have figured out a reason to keep it.

"Sounds like I think I know where Ben's going on his next vacation," Ian jested, his joke landing like a lead weight.

"No, we stick to the plan. I'm still gonna get those radios out there. They might just not be in the same place," Ben said contemplatively. "I'm going to get cleaned up and get the maps out. Wait till you two see these things."

Just when Ben thought he could take no more, another bell chimed throughout the house. The three of them looked at each other.

"Doorbell," Ben informed them. He walked over to the counter and picked up his pistol holster, putting it on and looking at the other two concerned people.

"Think the water shorted it?" Ian asked, following suit.

The cameras weren't working, and all the windows were

shuttered. Ben walked to the door, looking through the peephole to see a man with a hood on.

"Ben, you there?" came the voice from the other side. The person knew Ben.

This morning was starting to fray Ben's nerves. After a year of perfect bliss, shit had started piling up faster than he could pick it up.

"Yeah, who is this?" Ben asked with an edge in his voice.

"It's Jim, your neighbor from a few houses down. Jesus, man, let me in. I've been traveling for months. Thank God you're alive," Jim said as Ben pulled out his pistol before opening the door.

The man was dirty, his clothes torn. He lowered his hood, smiling, showing yellowing teeth.

"You alone?" Ben asked, not giving the man an inch.

"Yes, I was with some folks, but they didn't make it. You know how things are." That was the last thing Jim would ever say.

Jim took a step forward as Ben shot the man directly between the eyes. The high-velocity ammunition deconstructed the man's head in a spatter of gore and chunks.

Blood erupted from the man's brain, painting the front porch. Ben walked up to him, putting another round in the man's heart for good measure as one of his eyes popped out, landing by his foot.

The violence was swift and immediate. Ian and Kelly backed off, the click of Ian's pistol resonating behind Ben.

"Jesus, Jesus," Kelly was repeating as Ben turned around.

"You need to put that down," Ian demanded, holding up his own gun.

Ben took a calming, clearing breath, putting the pistol on the ground by the door.

"Step back," Ian ordered as he looked at Kelly.

"You better have a damn good reason why you just did that shit," Ian said, his eyes not moving.

"I do."

"What justifies that?" Kelly demanded.

"You know that house I told you not to go into?" Ben said,

noting it was not the one with Mrs. Brinkman in it.

Ian was squinting at Ben, trying to read him. "The one you didn't want to talk about. So what? Nothing justifies that. I thought you were all new world army, doing shit the right way. We trusted you!" He was raising his voice.

The peace and celebration from the message he had just received washed away as thoughts of what Ben had found in that house came to his mind. "He deserved worse."

Ian's and Kelly's nerves were also frayed after the past few days' events. Tempers started flaring as if someone had pushed the accelerator of a rumbling V8 engine all the way to the floorboard.

"Is that all you're going to say? What, the guy had better grass than you?" Kelly's age was showing.

With a sigh, Ben looked at Ian. "There's a pair of zip ties in the kitchen. Go get them. Tie me up, go to the house. Take the portable DVD player in my room with you. There's a false door in the closet of the master bedroom that man used to live in. You'll figure it out from there," Ben said, trailing off.

Ian and Kelly looked at each other, confused. They had known Ben for only a few days, but they had trusted him.

Ten minutes later, Ian and Kelly marched Ben to the front of the house. They avoided the front porch, walking through the standing water to get to the front gate.

Ben didn't say a word. Ian tied him to the gate within eyeshot of the house as Kelly stood several feet away holding her rifle. Neither wanted to be left alone with him.

Ben, on the other hand, was impressed with how fast they had reacted to the situation, not accepting the violence. He was sure they would soon deem it justified.

Ian started walking to the neighbor's house, radio on just in case, leaving Kelly to stand guard over Ben. They stood there in silence.

Thoughts of Sarah's message swam through Ben's mind. He was tempted, if released, to leave immediately for Tallahassee, but the plan was in place to avoid star-crossed lovers from missing each other en route to different locations.

Twenty minutes later, Ian returned, his head hanging down as he walked up to Ben, pulling out his knife. Kelly pulled up the rifle. Ian didn't look at her as he cut Ben loose without hesitation. The two men looked at each other, both knowing that what he had done had been justified.

"What is it?" Kelly asked, looking at the two men, silent understanding filling the air.

Ian walked over and gave Kelly a hug. "I love you, babe. We're in a good place."

Kelly looked over at Ben.

"I'll get the mess cleaned up. Sorry about that. I want to check out the area just in case. I'm sure he had some things on him," was all Ben said, walking off and leaving the two standing there.

"Hey, when are we going to get those battery cores or whatever you called them?" Ian asked in a raised voice to catch Ben as he walked away.

"Today," Ben replied.

EPILOGUE

"Damn piece of shit satellite," Sarah said as she turned the phone on, crossing her fingers. For once, the gods must have been listening as the prompt for a message glowed green on the screen, showing the data encryption key.

"You okay in there?" John asked through the closed door.

"I'm fine," Sarah replied, running to the corner of her room and throwing a blanket over her head to muffle the conversation she was so desperately trying to have.

Sarah's room was on the top floor of the Capitol building, several stories above the chaos below. The space was reserved for people the "Court" deemed important.

Sarah Hatton hadn't told them what kind of doctor she was, just that she was one. In all fairness, she did have a medical background. The Court didn't want people as valuable as Sarah to leave, working to keep her either busy or not interested in leaving.

The team she had been with since Denver had made great time to the Sunshine State, a little under three months from when they'd narrowly escaped the bunker, only to hit several obstacles in rapid succession.

One night, ten miles outside of Tallahassee, a mob of fresh crazies overran the building they'd been staying in. The gun battle and violence that followed had been breathtaking, one for the ages. After two days of the siege, a large group of people had shown up, saving what was left of Sarah's team.

Sarah, Nicole, Andrew, and Michael were all that was left of the once thirty strong Denver team, which had now been diminished to nothing more than a skeleton of its former self.

Sarah had convinced the crew in Denver that heading East toward the CDC headquarters in Atlanta was the best option they had. The team had left Denver a month after the evacuations had started, and the world had ground to a halt. Denver had been quickly overrun due to the weather and location. It hadn't been a hard sale for Sarah to convince the others to leave.

The CDC headquarters in Atlanta could support the group. Her plan, however, had been to peel off and head to Jacksonville instead of taking the turn north onto I-75. She had kept that part of the plan to herself though.

She had been, in a way, using the group, but her hunch about Atlanta was also a logical choice. They had access to systems there, and all of them knew they could stay as long as needed. Even with a group as large as theirs, the place had been made for this type of event.

Nicole was from Florida. Orlando, to be precise. She had been a transplant. The other two remaining survivors of her crew, Andrew and Michael, had both coincidentally grown up in Tennessee.

Due to their forced extended stay with the group in Tallahassee, she had trusted Nicole with her plan. She had been on board as well and had kept her secret. They would go to Jacksonville together, and from there, Nicole would head south to Orlando.

After the violent night on the outskirts of Tallahassee, they had gone to the capital to find a growing city of survivors. Sarah estimated the group to be roughly a thousand strong at the time. Things had changed throughout the last couple of months, with the numbers going up at times and at others mysteriously shrinking.

The conditions were decent compared to the rest of the country they had traveled through. For people like Sarah, it was another story. She had her pick of the rations, a good room, power, and even a private guard, same as the other special guests of the Court.

It had been made truly clear to Sarah that her services were desperately needed. For the first month, Sarah had done everything she could to help the group that had saved her life and that of her remaining friends. Since then, she had been working out how to utilize the satellite phone, only having an intermittent signal. It was encrypted, and messages would sometimes only come in from Ben as a letter, or she could only send out a certain amount of words before the encryption went out.

An honest-to-God phone call was out of the question, or so she thought. Sarah figured that the encryption key was slowly slipping, and time was running out. What she did know was that Ben was alive and that they were sticking to the plan.

On the night that she had finally received a response back from Ben, she had prepared to leave only to be told that it wasn't safe. After another month, Sarah had figured out this "advice" was, in reality, their way of keeping her from leaving. The Court had decided that she would stay, and Sarah didn't know how to proceed.

But that had changed after a few people had come in from Jacksonville, telling of survivors. The Court hadn't considered the effect this may have on Sarah. It had motivated her to leave.

They had other things to worry about... The people in the Capitol were not a violent group but one of forced community. To be honest, she really didn't know what drove the leaders of the Court. She had even, at some point, considered a future here with Ben after they were reunited.

"It's working!" Sarah exclaimed, quickly putting her hand over her mouth.

She had a full signal. Bars, encryption, and all.

"Hey, you need me to come in there?" John asked again, obviously at the door. He had been assigned to guard her and other important guests, at least that's what the Court had said. As she had found out, he was really there to keep the important people where they needed to be.

Sarah had at one time even considered asking for his help, playing off his emotions since he obviously liked her. However, couldn't justify it due to the fact that she was being treated well. John was a genuinely nice person to boot.

Sarah quickly got off the phone as the door creaked lightly.

"Hey! Privacy, please," Sarah stressfully told John. "I'm just thinking out loud."

John was a good guy by all accounts. He dropped his eyes to the floor as he started shutting the door. "Hey, sorry. I'm just doing—"

"Doing your job, I know. Thanks, John. Good night. And could you stand by someone else's door?" Sarah said. The two chuckled lightly, easing the mood.

As she heard his footsteps echo down the hall, Sarah quickly picked up the satellite phone. She was shaking — trembling — as she rapidly pushed the buttons, putting the phone up to her ear and hearing the dial tone. Sarah quickly wrote down the exact time and location, including the cycle of the moon in case it was relevant to the satellite's orbit. She would figure this out.

The phone went to a generic voice mail that she knew as soon as Ben got any kind of signal, he would be able to listen to.

"My God, it's working. Oh, God. It only works at certain times in certain places, the satellites. Ben, I got your text. The plan. I'm getting close. I'm in Florida, but it's gotten complicated. Things are—" Static

The signal on the phone fizzled out as a droning beep filled Sarah's ear.

ACKNOWLEDGMENTS

Special thanks go out to all my family, friends, and the authors that still inspire me to do more.

To my family, my wife and two sons. This book is part of my legacy to you. When I am but a memory in time, you will always be able to pick this book up and remember what a nerd I really was and, well…still am…

P.S. Hey, Netflix…Call me…

BOOKS BY THIS AUTHOR

Max Abbaddon Series

URBAN FANTASY AT ITS FINEST.

AUDIOBOOKS NARRATED BY LUKE DANIELS

The Sinking Man Series

ZOMBIES!

AUDIOBOOKS NARRATED BY JARRET LEMASTER

www.ingramcontent.com/pod-product-compliance
Lightning Source LLC
Chambersburg PA
CBHW030633130626

46552CB00002B/835